The
Real Louise
and other stories

Also by Ailsa Cox

Writing Short Stories (Routledge)
Alice Munro (Northcote House)

To Jenn
Thanks for a great
reading
4/3/10

The
Real Louise
and other stories

AILSA COX

HEADLAND

First published in 2009
by
HEADLAND PUBLICATIONS
38 York Avenue, West Kirby,
Wirral, Merseyside. CH48 3JF

Copyright © 2009 AILSA COX

A full CIP record for this book is available
from the British Library

ISBN 978 1 902096 57 5

Printed in Great Britain by
Oriel Studios
Hawthorne Road, Liverpool L20 6NS

HEADLAND acknowledges the financial
assistance of Arts Council England.

CONTENTS

for Tom

ACKNOWLEDGEMENTS

'Biting Point' was originally published in *Northern Stories 2,* ed. Maura Dooley, Philip Callow, David Morley; 'Her Old Self Again' in *Red Ink*; 'Into the Sun' in *Metropolitan*; 'Making It Happen' in *London Magazine*; 'No Problemo' on *East of the Web*; '20th Frame' in *Stand One,* ed. Michael Blackburn, Jon Silkin, Lorna Tracy; 'Just Like Robert de Niro' in *Critical Quarterly* and *The Virago Book of Love and Loss*, ed. Georgina Hammick; 'Story Swap' in *Manchester Stories 3,* ed. Ra Page; 'The Memory Room' in *Transmission*; 'Be a Good Girl' in *Writing Women* and *Holding On* (Crocus Books); 'Doors of Tunis' on *Rainy City Stories.*

Thanks to the Research Development Fund at Edge Hill University, for funding the editing of this collection. Thanks are also due to the Narrative Research Group for their suggestions, to Elizabeth Baines, and to all those who, wittingly or unwittingly, have provided me with stories.

The introduction to Sefton Park in 'November' is taken from Joseph Sharples, *Liverpool* (Pesvener Architectural Guide, 2004).

BITING POINT

Mirror, handbrake, signal.

Never thought I'd learn to drive.

Never thought I was the type.

'Were you good at sport at school?'

'No, I was useless.'

'Usually, you find the ones that were good at games pick up driving pretty quick.' Janice folds her heavy arms. She's wearing a military-coloured body warmer. 'Find your biting point,' she says.

Janice is the size of an ammunition truck. I'm what you might call dainty. Or petite. Pint-sized. Or midget. I have to winch my seat towards the wheel. And then I spend the next half hour adjusting the mirror. Not that it makes any difference. I still can't see a thing.

The seatbelt is twisted. 'Oops, I'm sorry.' I smile at her, hating my own girlishness as I do so.

Janice watches without comment. But she was good at sport. She never dropped the ball. Her cakes never collapsed, nor her stitches unravelled. Her colours always stayed inside the lines.

She unwraps a mint without offering me one. From time to time, she will stick her tongue out, balancing the polo on its tip. I know Janice very well. I recognise the voices speaking through her.

'Handbrake!' she cries. 'You should know which way by now.'

High time you knew those equations. You can see me after school.

9

I struggle to subdue the handbrake, strangely like a male erection; and the gearstick too is disconcertingly penile.

'You're very heavy-handed.'

My best china! Honestly – you clumsy article!

'You're pulling with one hand! This hand's doing nothing! You'll never pass your test if you don't steer properly.

You won't get anywhere, Ms Higginbotham, till you change your attitude.

No, I never thought I'd drive a car till I was followed. I was coming home from Conversational German. Usually I get a lift from the tutor. But there's a new girl started. She's younger than me, and a few inches taller.

Komm schon, he says, we can squeeze you in, *so eine Kleine!*

No thanks. I dropped hints I was meeting some one. I intended to find a taxi, but the evening was so light it didn't seem necessary.

I loved this part of town when I first moved here – big old houses, once so grand, now decaying beauties standing on untended land. In spring, the trees are marshmallowed; when the blossom falls, green tunnels form the whole length of the streets. The only sound is the cooing of pigeons.

But peace can be misleading.

At first I wasn't sure I was really being followed. The long silver car crawled to a stop at the crossroads. Nothing was coming either way. It paused. I walked. It shadowed me. I didn't dare look round. I moved to the other pavement. I could see the distant vision of home, floating close to me above the trees.

'I said right after the crossroads! Don't indicate yet! Turn the wheel, tightly, turn the wheel!'

I work at the wheel for all my life's worth. I grind, I push, we've made it. My armpits are damp, and my back and my head.

'No need to force it,' she says.

Peace is dangerous – quiet roads more threatening than the noisy streets near pubs. The sky was darkening, ready for a rainstorm. The thick, concealing trees were now a menace. There was no one to help me. I walked as fast as I could, swinging my keys as if the act of holding them brought me closer to my flat. I slipped inside the door, opening the barest crack before I bolted it behind me.

From the first floor, I could see the car, parked like a silver fish outside the gateway, and the shadow of a man behind the wheel.

'Take next left. That's better. Did you do what I said? Did you practice with a plate?'

I sat by the phone, trying to think who to call. It lay there like a toad, and then, when it rang of its own accord, I screamed and jumped.

'What's up?' said Dad. 'You sound on edge.'

'Do I? I must be a little bit tired.'

'Did I get you out of bed? I'm sorry, chuck. Only I rang before and there was no answer. Seemed a bit strange. You don't usually go out on a Monday.'

I didn't contradict.

'Thought I'd better check you were alright. You never know. You read some terrible things in the paper.'

'Don't be silly. It's nothing like as bad as they make out. In fact, this street is really peaceful.'

'I called in the solicitor's… You only have to say the word.

He said there'd be no problem putting the house in your name. It's what your mother would have wanted.'

'Yes, I know, and I have been thinking about it. I'll ring you tomorrow Dad, I'm tired now. Tomorrow.'

For the first time in my life, that house seemed like a refuge. The plastic shields round the light switches, the smell of furniture polish, the porch where my mother asked the guests to leave their shoes – all of this began to seem quite tempting.

When I put the phone down, the car had disappeared. As I checked the locks on all my windows, I thought, I'm sick of this. I thought, I wish I could escape. I wish I could jump in a car and just go where I wanted, scarcely making the decision. I wished I didn't have to stay indoors when it gets dark.

'Fourth gear.'

I'm trapped here. Here, which is there, exposed on this gigantic dual carriageway. Cars are aiming at me like bullets from a gun. Killers aiming at me, every one.

What's Janice saying? Something about work, about weekends, holidays. Hairdresser's conversation. She's trying to relax me. I can't speak. I'm going too fast. They're aiming at me, all these vehicles are out to kill me.

I thought: if I had my own car. If only I could drive. I'd never be afraid.

Nothing to be scared of! You're a big girl! You can do it! Take a deep breath now – and go!

But I can't. I'll never swim. I'm scared of water. It wasn't my fault, honestly, Dad, not as if I didn't try. Marina was the sporty one, not me. You just assumed we were the same.

All that has changed since Mum died.

'I do worry, you know,' he says. 'I worry about you.'

'How's your dad?' asks Janice as we, mercifully, reach the traffic lights. 'Brake gently – and stop. Into first gear.'

'The same.' I'm gasping for air. I was holding my breath all the time we were out there. 'Ten years older every time I see him. He shuffles. He's losing weight – won't cook for himself. Says there's no point, and that's when it starts. Soon as you try to talk, he passes hints, more than hints. He's talking overdoses, tower blocks.'

Well, I have to tell some one.

Janice pokes her tongue out, with the polo mint stuck on the end.

I'm watching the lights, their colours bright as tranquillisers.

'So, did you make your decision?'

Before I can answer, I'm moving again – with a stutter – but at least I didn't tussle with the handbrake. I cancel my signal, change gear without prompting. I dip round the parked cars, and back into lane. I feel good.

You see? You can do it. You just don't want to succeed.

It's a clear, cold day. If I had a car, I'd drive to the sea – somewhere on a cliff edge. I'd sling what I needed straight into the boot. No need for calculating suitcase loads – the minimum I need versus the most I can carry. I don't have to decide between shoes. I can take the lot! No more draughty railway stations, no more waiting at bus stops. I wouldn't have to look out the window before I get dressed in the morning. I wouldn't have to keep an umbrella with me. My little motor. What sort shall I get?

'Keep your speed up.'

But I'm already going fast.

My little motor, something nippy, continental, rather chic. A sun roof. I don't need a lot of room, just enough space for myself. And possibly one more passenger.

I grasp the rounded gearstick passionately.

A special passenger. If I could find him.

'Don't hesitate! The road's clear! Straight across!'

Or I could go for an English eccentric – a Morris Minor or Triumph Herald. No, I'd look like an old maid. If I'm choosing a two-seater, why not buy a sports car? Hop in, I'd say, dropping sunglasses. I'll take you for a spin. Okay, why not? He leaps aboard.

Without even thinking, I've tamed the car. I can feel it riding smoothly underneath me, responding like a lover. We're in love.

I'll be my own woman, smartly slamming the car door, swirling the keys in her hand, striding through the gate.

The gateway to a house which is not my parents' house. My shoes are staying on my feet.

I've always wanted to be grown up. I used to think it would happen when I was allowed to wear tights instead of socks; and then my periods started; and then when I lost my virginity; and now here I am, nearly forty, and my brains still caught in pigtails.

There are three doors into growing up – mortgage, marriage and a motor. Everyone goes through them, sooner or later. Nearly everyone.

I've been in love. Then he got divorced from his wife, and he married my sister Marina.

I can see Marina now, immaculate behind the wheel, driving a VW Polo into the double garage. I've never earned enough to buy a house. Why don't I get myself promoted? I work hard. But I don't get it right. Other people overtake me all the time. Is it my attitude?

When I've passed my test, I'll apply for other jobs. All the money I'm spending on lessons, is an investment; it's another qualification. I could commute.

I have reached a crossroads. My whole life is changing now.

If I buy a car, I can reach Dad when he needs me. But I don't have to move in. I can get a place of my own, somewhere in the country.

Janice suddenly flattens the brake. She seizes the wheel from my hands. 'You just don't look, do you? That car was coming straight towards us. Come on, concentrate! You're in a world of your own!'

Daydreaming, Ms Higginbotham?

A tendency to daydream. She must make an effort to concentrate next term.

Did you hear, Ms Higginbotham? I said, we are waiting for coffee.

You drive a car? That's a daft idea for starters.

My mother has come from the grave. When Janice opens her mouth, it's her voice that's hissing in my ear.

And what's this latest? A cottage? Out there? Miles away from anyone?

I can't hear what Janice is trying to tell me.

You and your half-baked schemes. Living in that flat. You know what it's like round there. I can't see the sense of it, not when you've got a nice home with us.

Her voice is changing now, deepening like my dad's

15

voice. Now it's beating from within me, seductive and relentless, another voice altogether.

Give up. Lie down and die. You will never learn to drive. You'll never grow up. You should never have got your own place.

'Are you listening?' Janice taps my knee. 'I'm speaking to you.'

Go back to your father. What else are you good for? Watch him grow senile. You'll give up your job. Eventually you'll die.

'Turn the wheel like *this*, I've told you a hundred times. You were doing it right before. Then all of a sudden you go back again.'

'Yes, I know.'

No one will ever love you. Give up. Lie down and die.

'Never turn a corner in third gear! What's the matter with you?'

'I don't know.'

'Never ever cut a corner!'

Never love you.

'If you cut corners, you'll never pass your test.'

'I didn't intend to. I'm sorry.'

'It's no good being sorry, is it?'

That won't mend the vase.

'You don't even try.'

Come on, give it a try! Show your daddy what you can do!

Must try harder. Must try harder. Make more effort. You'll never get anywhere if you don't try.

'It's no good,' I say. 'I'm hopeless. I'll never get anywhere. I'm not cut out for this.' I lean on the steering wheel, almost embracing it in my longing for comfort. The horn blares like the trumpet of doom.

'Oh, I'm sorry, I'm always doing that, I'm so stupid!'

Janice takes my appointment card from the dashboard. She folds my cheque and licks her biro. 'What you need is practice. Isn't there anyone who can take you out for an hour or two?'

She's asked me this before. She knows the answer is no.

Because no one gives a damn. No one's going to lay his car keys at your feet. No one will love you.

'Shall we say Thursday same time?'

'Is there any point in this? Am I ever going to learn?'

'Well now,' says Janice. 'How many lessons have you had?'

'I don't know.' I don't want to count the weeks, or the money either. I've giving up going for drinks with the girls in the office. Now I stay at home, practising my steering on a plate. Two lessons a week since Spring – it's November now.

'Anyone can learn to drive,' she says. 'Anyone. With time.'

With time. Bolted to the wheel without parole, never flinching, never doubting, anyone can pass. Any fool except this idiot. Me, of all the people in the world. How easy it is to them all. As simple as breathing, as natural as digestion. As normal as adolescence. So why am I different? It's as if I was born without lungs or a stomach.

Misery, oh misery. I'm sitting in the car in some unknown part of suburbia. I've no memory of arriving. I drove here, I suppose. I sit tamely in the backseat, while Janice thumps on the door of a semi. Cars go back and forth, driven by those perfect others, the ones who passed the test.

Us kids jumped into the car, soon as Mum and Dad were gone. ('Just sit quietly. We won't be a minute.') We rotated the steering wheel. Vroom vroom! We tooted the horn naughtily.

Dad drove. Mum balanced the map on her lap. 'No, I said turn left after the second set of lights.'

'You should have said it quicker, there's traffic behind me!'

'I did say, I told you back there. If you'd gone the way I said, we wouldn't be stuck in this traffic. But you never listen to me. You always think you know best. Same as this flaming motor. Told you, you were buying rubbish. We'll be lucky if it gets us to Scarborough.'

'Belt up Gladys, keep your mind on the bloody map.'

'I can't see a damn thing, you're driving too fast! You'll get us all killed!'

'What's my speed got to do with it? You need bloody glasses!'

'You and your language, a fine example you are!'

I can see her eyes tense in the mirrored sunshield. Then suddenly she turns round and yells.

'Will you kids stop whining! I told you, didn't I, I told you to use the toilet before we came. We're not stopping the car now. You'll have to hold it.'

And he says, 'Where am I going? Tell me, where am I going?'

The next client is a long lad, scarcely old enough to shave. He nods, and slides the seat way back till I'm crushed almost into the boot. The car drives smoothly into the traffic.

'Have a polo, Maurice?' Janice says.

He leans back dreamily. His hands are gentle on the wheel. The car swings easily around a roundabout.

'How'd you get on Thursday?' Janice asks.

Soon they're talking busily about all kinds of mysterious social events. Janice is actually smiling at him. And he still never falters. The gear stick swells within his grasp.

I don't know how I'll get through work today. My back hurts with the tension of driving; and my head aches when I look at the plate glass of Mazda House shining high above the other office blocks. Unanswered letters are stuffed at the back of my desk. The phone's ringing at reception. *Where's she got to?* Men in suits are reading watches. *Try to be on time in future.*

Not Maurice's fault – how could he do wrong? – but two miles from the centre, we're already caught in roadworks. I rub at the steamy glass. Marina and me used to write our names backwards for the traffic jams to read.

Marina rang last night. 'I don't know why you're hesitating. Why pay rent when you could have that house? I hope you realise, it's a sacrifice for me. I shan't get anything now. But what can I do? I've a family to see to. You're alright. You don't have responsibilities.'

I said nothing. I was practising the highway code.

'How're the driving lessons? Poor Dad, he loved his car. He's getting too old for it now. That Escort hasn't been out of the garage since the day of the funeral. He told me you can have it, soon as you pass your test. You can take him for a spin, get him out of the house for a change.'

'He could do the map reading.'

'Yes!' she cried, delighted. 'Do you both the world of good!'

Stuck behind an enormous, dusty lorry. Maurice taps the steering wheel, already a real driver. My Dad used to do that. In exactly the same tones, he'd mutter, 'Come on, come ON.'

For the first time this morning, I take a look around me. The city's quilted with metal on metal, the vehicles so close they're welded to one flesh. Somewhere a siren screams. A helicopter's moaning overhead.

'Come on, you stupid...get a move on, can't you?' Maurice curses. In the car next to us, a woman's hunched over the wheel. She turns her head as I watch her. Her eyes are desperate.

And a new voice speaks: Give up.

I try to harden myself. I try not to listen. Then I realise, this voice has nothing to do with Janice. Or my parents or schoolteachers or the men at Mazda House. I don't know where it comes from. It simply says: Give up. You don't have to do any of this. Then it falls silent again. There's no bullying, no cajoling, no deep, deadly seduction.

My parents are still there, of course, squashed with me in the back. He says, 'All that money you wasted on lessons. You can't give up now.'

She says, 'You can't stick at anything, can you? Oh well then, another daft scheme bites the dust.'

I don't say anything. Apart from: 'Let me out.'

They carry on talking. 'Just like the ballet lessons' – 'She was too clumsy, that's why, she isn't they type' – 'Why can't she find the right attitude?' – 'Like the horse riding, the piano, Marina can, why can't she?'

'Drop me off here,' I say, much louder. I'll walk the rest of the way.'

Mirror, handbrake, signal. The car is re-absorbed into the spinal cord of traffic. I can hardly breathe for fumes.

Mazda House rears up before me, the tallest building in the city. Is this where you were going, Dad? Is this where you thought you might throw yourself off, if you didn't choose pills or the rope? 'At least I'll be with Gladys, wherever she's gone.'

Not if she was map reading, you wouldn't.

By the doors of Mazda House, a long, low silver car, like a metal fish, is parked. There's no one inside but you can tell it's a man's car.

You'll never learn.

So what?

I push at the revolving door.

You can't do anything.

Oh yes I can. I just can't drive, that's all.

Attitude, Ms Higginbotham, attitude.

I spin the glass door hard, and stride back along the pavement, scraping my keys along the silver car. Suddenly I feel much taller. Graceful now, and womanly, I raise my hand in the air, and hail myself a taxi like the grown ups.

INTO THE SUN

Storm clouds are gathering over the dry land. All across Baghdad, the lamps are turned out. In Manchester, Jessie's desperate for daylight. The station's one long windy tunnel, like wintertime itself.

Clio's started whining. 'When's he coming? I'm freezing cold, Mum.'

'I told you, find your gloves.'

'I hate them. They make me itch.'

'For God's sake, can you hear yourself? You sound more like three than thirteen.'

DO NOT LEAVE BAGGAGE UNATTENDED – PASSENGERS ARE ADVISED THAT THE LEFT LUGGAGE LOCKERS ARE TEMPORARILY OUT OF SERVICE – ANY SUSPICIOUS PACKAGES SHOULD BE REPORTED TO THE STATION SUPERVISOR

At home the central heating's turned up, the radiators newly stripped of underwear. There are clean towels in the bathroom, fragrant with conditioner. All the old newspapers have been chucked into the bin; so have the dusty jars that never reached the bottle bank. The shelves are re-stocked with chocolate biscuits, croissants and fresh coffee. Nobody asked Jessie to go to the shops or to stay up late cleaning. Nobody made her invite Paul to Clio's concert. The truth is, she never thought he'd have the time.

'Can't we go in the buffet? It's freezing out here.'

A January day in 1991. War clouds are gathering over the desert. All across Baghdad, the lamps are rubbed out. An explosion. Blood and panic. Dead before the cup hits the saucer.

Dead without knowing. The child's body mashed into history. A package left under a table. A parcel dropped from the sky. The lamps are out. So many lives will soon be gone. Why should this special life be spared, sucking Pepsi through a straw?

'What's the matter with you, Mum? Stop touching me all the time. You get on my nerves.' Clio flicks the straight yards, furlongs and cubits of her hair. She pokes at her drink with the straw. 'Why do I have to sleep with you?'

Jessie lifts her cup again. 'We've been through all of this. If you don't want to get into bed with me there's always the spare mattress.'

'Why can't Dad have the spare mattress in my room? Then I can be with him.'

'You know why.'

'Oh yeah, my dad's going to molest me...'

'You know I'm saying nothing of the kind. It isn't suitable. You know that.'

THE TRAIN NOW ARRIVING ON PLATFORM SIX IS THE DELAYED 13.06 FROM LONDON EUSTON. THIS TRAIN TERMINATES HERE.

Jessie hasn't seen Paul for a while, not since Clio started travelling to London by herself. ('You will be careful, won't you? Speak to the guard if anyone pesters you.') He's lost some more hair and the plush overcoat adds bulk. But she'd know him anywhere, even without Clio shrieking in his arms. Jessie and Paul were an unlikely pair – the lean and sombre man; the plump, loud-voiced woman, the sort that's supposed to be jolly. The girls who wanted to steal him thought they'd be restoring a balance.

The wind slams into the three of them, as they leave the

station, forcing their way through the tide of commuters. Jessie tries to catch a glimpse of the hoardings. Are we at war yet? She wants to know exactly when it starts, just as they knew in 1939, huddled round the wireless.

I HAVE TO TELL YOU NOW THAT NO SUCH UNDERTAKING HAS BEEN RECEIVED.

Paul taps her shoulder. 'Wait a minute, Jess. Aren't we taking a taxi?'

'What for? The bus goes in ten minutes.'

Clio rolls her eyes.

CONSEQUENTLY THIS COUNTRY IS AT WAR.

'Mum says I have to sleep with her because you might molest me.'

Sometimes Jessie catches herself watching from the corner of the room. The other Jessie folds her arms and says, 'If she were mine, I'd smack her bottom.'

Coffee drips onto the schoolbook she's meant to be marking. She wipes it with her sleeve.

Paul noticed that.

She writes *See me* at the bottom of Matthew Bennett's essay, and throws it on the floor with a deep sigh. She's still tired from last night's cleaning. Her mind's on other things, the war for instance – has it started? The radio was full of vague predictions, speculation, fuzzy correspondents choked with expectation. When she closes her eyes, young men parade behind the lids, their waxen faces those of Matthew Bennett, Darren Smith, Ben Reed. What passing-bells for those who die as cattle? *Spelling please!!!* she underlines in red. She targets stray apostrophes, as if it really matters. Gas! Gas! Quick boys!

Clio's whispering in Paul's ear. Like she whispers with her

friend Rachel, giggling down the phone, hanging round the Arndale on a Saturday afternoon. The silk dress she chose last time she went to London has been dumped on the floor, like a rain-flattened rose – right next to the flute, also paid for by Paul. She changed her clothes in front of him without self-consciousness. Her body's as straight as the long hair that shields it, slender as a blade of grass – except for her breasts. The new dress does nothing to hide them.

Jessie never had best friends. She was too fat. She made them laugh, didn't she? That way, people didn't mind her being clever. Mimicking the teachers when they turned to use the board, she never dreamt that she herself was going to turn into a schoolmarm.

'Time you were off to bed.'

'Ohh...' The constipated squirm, the squeezed-up nose. 'It's not fair. I'm wide awake.' The flounce. 'She makes me go too early. She treats me like a kid. I can't even watch TV. I'm the only one in our class who hasn't seen *Twin Peaks*.'

Paul sits smiling faintly from Jessie's armchair.

'I don't want to go to bed. I need to talk to Dad. Oh, don't be tight.'

'You need your rest. It's a big day tomorrow. You wouldn't want to let him down.'

'Is he allowed to tuck me in?'

'Don't forget to hang that dress up.'

'Not now, I'm so tired! Can't you do it, Mum?'

Paul was Jessie's best friend. They were mates. They knew each other in the dark.

THE LATEST NEWS FROM THE GULF – WE'RE GETTING UNCONFIRMED REPORTS – A BOMBING

RAID ON ISRAEL

Up to her elbows in suds, she tries to follow what they're saying. The washing up's just an excuse to listen to the radio. She ought to be finishing her marking. No time tomorrow, not with Clio's concert. She rinses the plates in slow motion. There have been no declarations, no steps closer to war. You just wake up and it's happening, like middle age, like the death of love, as if it was always like this.

'Shall I make more coffee Jess?' Paul has a Radio Four voice these days, the suave male voice of authority. Not his real voice – the way he was, hunched over his desk, lean as the anglepoise. Two a.m. Drunken first years in the distance. On the other side of the wall, a woman panting: 'Yes yes yes, oh no, yes please, oh yes…'

'Coffee Jess,' he'd say, 'I can't think…' when he'd already got some, and Jessie shifting the mug closer to his arm locked around a book. *The Waste Land. Ulysses.* 'Any chocolate biscuits, Jess?' Head down, guarding A4 feint with margin. Buried in his foxhole, not feeling her touch.

Next door louder still. 'Yes, yes!'

'Christ!' Banging the wall. 'Fucking shut up!'

Not his desk at all, Jessie's – Jessie's room. When Jessie tries to write an essay, she tips the chair back on two legs and sits staring at the poster, *Hylas and the Nymphs.* The nymphs look like they're asking to be let out of the water, rather than enticing him in. They could do with a cup of cocoa. Their breasts are cold as ice cream, with the nipples painted out. Who was Hylas anyway? What's it supposed to be about? Jessie's given up on essays. No point now, is there? If there ever was a point.

She's lying on the bed, flicking through knitting patterns. This is the first time she's ever tried to knit. Her mother can't bear to sit idle, without needles in her hands; she said to Jessie so many times, you should learn to knit, make yourself useful for a change. Now she is learning – not her mother's way, but from a book. What she meant to do tonight was write a letter home. She's decided that's all wrong – better tell them face to face. But she can't bear that either. Write, then visit. Write a letter in the morning. Jessie's tired. Needs to rest, in her condition. But Paul's still deep inside his foxhole; how can she sleep without him next to her?

Something real is happening inside Jessie. Something real, not like all that sifting and balancing, the weighing of opinions about insubstantial words, thoughts breathed by writers buried long ago.

Jessie was always top at school. At university, she's one of many. Paul's after a first. Big deal. Save getting a job, she supposes, if he stays on. But when Paul wants something, he gets a hunger for it. He just can't stop himself. He'd like them to get married. But what's the point? What's it supposed to prove? It's how you feel that matters, not the piece of paper.

The nymphs had hair like Clio's, a sheer drop into the pool. It's a long time since Jessie's thoughts lingered in that poky student room. When she goes back into the lounge, it seems suddenly darker. She has to switch on the main light.

'Aren't you watching telly?' She clicks the zapper.

'Hmm?' Paul's busy by the bookcase. As he bends over, the spotlight on the shelf polishes his bald patch.

'Don't you want to know what's going on?' The families gathered round the wireless. Mother knitting. Father smokes his pipe.

'Isn't this one of mine?' He picks out a dusty Wilfred Owen. 'Yes, here's my name on the flyleaf.'

'You took all your books.'

'In pencil, you can just about see it.'

'We did the War Poets in the first term. We weren't sharing then. We would have had one each. If I've got yours, you've probably got mine. So we're even.'

She stands there, smoothing Clio's dress, watching the model landscape on TV, each empty space labelled – KUWAIT – IRAQ – waiting for a train set or some plastic dinosaurs. Then the soldiers come on screen, lads speaking with Lancashire accents. Some one's got to fight, it's just a job, it's what we're trained for. Not sad, nor proud, nor curious at all.

'It wasn't the first term. It was the start of the second year. This one's mine.'

'What does it matter!' A folded sheet of notes flutters loose as she snatches the book from his hands.

'Mine,' he says, grabbing it from the floor. 'See, I told you.'

'Take it, I don't care.'

'Just making the point. But if you don't mind, I'd like to borrow it tonight.' He glances briefly at the television. 'What's happening then? Has World War Three started?'

'Don't say that. Don't even use those words.'

'Not with a bang, but with a whimper. Oh, chocolate digestives!' His wrists seem very hairy as they dip inside the tin. 'Haven't eaten those in years. You're treating me very well, Jess. You didn't have to cook: I could've taken us out.'

He's remembering lentils, carrots and brown rice, soured

28

by the scent of Clio's nappies. Thank God she finally learnt how to cook. He hasn't seen the Marks and Spencer cartons pushed carefully to the bottom of the bin. Jessie smiles at the thought, and he smiles back at her. She's about to ask him if he knows who Hylas was when voices are raised, music blares, something else is happening.

The end of February, and the sun's come back, like a light switched on. Suddenly you don't need to wear two jumpers any more. Jessie's garden explodes with crocus and daffodil. The spring light shows up the dirt, the greasy kitchen rime, the grey smeared windows. Time for Jessie's blitz.

'Does it have to be now? I'll do it later.' Clio's swept from her bed before the words are even out.

'I've vacuumed downstairs,' Jessie tells her, handing over the Ajax. 'You can go over the doors and skirting boards.'

'What for, why?'

'I'll inspect what you've done when I've finished in here.'

'No, you've had your chance. I asked you enough times, for instance when Paul was coming'

'I tidied up for him'

'Huh.'

'Yes I did.'

'Look, save it. I'll stick the rubbish in a bin liner. You can have a look through before it goes out. Come on, down those stairs! Get to work!'

Jessie starts picking up the torn magazines, crisp packets, cassettes without a case. She plugs in the radio, THIS IS NO VIETNAM, wrenching hairs from Clio's matted brush. THE PROPHETS OF DOOM HAVE BEEN WRONG – THESE

MEN WILL BE RETURNING HOME AS HEROES. The urbane voices run into one another, predicting, commentating, while Jessie sets about her scorched-earth policy, thrusting rubbish into one black bag, underclothes into another.

The war is over, if there ever was a war. Matthew Bennett, Darren Smith, Ben Reed, will sit their exams. The luggage lockers at the station will soon be back in service. Jessie will stop waking up whenever a plane passes.

Schoolbooks go into the desk, which Clio has converted into a dressing table, an exact reversal of Jessie's own behaviour at thirteen. The Wilfred Owen seems out of place, until she remembers. Paul was right; you can just trace his name on the flyleaf.

Last night she dreamt about a charred figure, his fingers still splayed on the wheel of the jeep, his skin roasted like burnt sugar.

Paul should have stuck to his research. He loved books. There's more to him, she's sure of it, than what he is now. So what if he only got a 2:1? He was up to it, everyone knew that. The baby, disruption, was just an excuse. Alright, Jessie told him, move out why don't you? See how you get on without me.

Bolt upright, a grin without a face, a tarred and naked body.

Six months later, Paul comes back, cropped and trimmed in shiny shoes. Says he's chucked it all in for a job in advertising. She says, you're kidding, aren't you? He says he's done it for Jessie and Clio, for the three of them. They can have a house together, no more cramped and mouldy basements. Paul wants to work. He wants to make something of himself. It's a job, that's all. Some one's going to rake it in, so why not him?

She supposed it was creative, in a way. But he just laughed at that. That was what made her mind up, the braying laugh. He wasn't like himself. Nowadays it's no great sin to work in advertising. Everybody's up for sale these days. Even Jessie's school puts out a glossy leaflet. The Labour Party's got a logo now. Paul's not so bad. He cares about Clio. If it wasn't for him nagging at her, she'd never have kept up her practice. Supposing Jessie had made a different decision, what sort of life would they be living?

ON THE ROAD TO BASRA – THE PITIFUL REMAINS OF SADDAM'S ARMY

She sighs as she picks up the overflowing bin. The whole place is a mess. It needs decorating – maybe Easter? Clio can help. She's always complaining that she's got nothing to do. Paul won't have time for her. He flies off somewhere romantic in April, him and that skinny young wife.

A TURKEY SHOOT – LIKE CATTLE IN A PEN

She switches the radio off. She doesn't want to think about it. What passing-bells, what passing-bells…All over the desert, fires blaze into the night. The stench sticks to your throat, like tar, like burning rubber, rancid fat. Smoke hangs heavy in the air.

Paul offered to buy her a dishwasher, the night before the concert. She knew he felt sorry for her, slaving away in her dark northern terrace. But for Jessie these are the good days, the times she looked forward to when she went back to college. There's nothing left to aspire to, at least not for herself. She had to turn him down, she didn't have the space.

Those are pearls that were his eyes. A TURKEY SHOOT – THE PITIFUL REMAINS. The lamps are blown out all over

Baghdad. Blue flames are roaring in the distance. Jessie hoovers under the bed, pushing the metal nozzle, trying not to think about anything else.

Paul squeezes one final cup from his cafetiére. He's the only one who can finish this off. He knows exactly what he's aiming for, just there, creeping over the horizon. The words inch onto the screen.

> *Courage is ours, and we have mystery*
> *Wisdom is ours, and we have mastery*

He hunches forwards, as if to embrace his machine. The cursor's bobbing, ready to go. His hand hesitates on the mouse. Too fancy, perhaps? No, this is the moment for grandeur, the war cleanly won, the technology proven. A thousand rounds a minute. Beautiful.

THE NEW ATTILA FXS –
THE POETRY IS IN THE POWER

That's it. Done. Just the gun itself for the visuals, filling the whole frame, in black and white, or maybe brown, like sepia but stronger, darker. Paul uncurls from his machine and looks out of the window for the first time today. It's already dark outside, much later than he thought. The streets are inky underneath the bluish city lights. As he tidies away the photos and the scribbled drafts, he can smell his wife's cooking. Italian tonight. Stop off for the olives on his way home. Clio ate olives last time she came, aubergines too. Her taste is improving. He liked the way she went straight for the silk when she picked out a dress for her concert. She looked good in it too. She has style. A pretty girl like her, she could play the flute professionally. He can see her on the album covers. Maybe she ought to come to

Rome with them this Easter. Do her good to spend some time abroad.

Paul takes one last look before he switches off the lights. Everything's in order, everything's in place, waiting for him to come back tomorrow.

HER OLD SELF AGAIN

I used to hate going home. I still called Manchester home, though I'd been living somewhere else for seven years. I was grown up, with a proper job and not just a boyfriend, a husband-to-be. Yet part of me was still a little half-baked student. During the holidays I went back and slept in my old room. It never crossed my mind to stay away.

Home was inevitable, like exams used to be. My real life was suspended as I sat on my mother's saggy settee, answering questions and eating too much. It was like being laid up with a mild dose of flu. Being looked after wasn't so bad – not after coping with a class of six year olds. And utter boredom has its compensations, when you've just been dragged through OFSTED. What I really dreaded about going home was Nanna.

My mother put it all down to her age. But when was Nanna any different? She'd always been the same, scowling over Sunday dinner, re-folding her serviette or peering at the knives. She had a different pair of glasses for every purpose. Sometimes she used their lenses like a magnifying glass, to look for eyes in boiled potatoes. 'Did you wash this plate?' 'Where'd you get the meat from?' 'These carrots aren't cooked.'

Nanna had always been old. She disliked young people, and she never took to children. They were messy, rooting creatures, more animal than human. I knew this instinctively when I was small. I felt Nanna flinch as she offered her cheek for a kiss; my lips barely touched the scented surface, powdered like a cake with icing sugar.

Nanna was the bad fairy. All her gifts were poisoned. My old bedroom was filled with fragile piggy banks, fiddly craft sets and costume dolls still under cellophane (too good to play with). I still cracked cups, lost scarves and bracelets that would have been safe if they weren't presents from Nanna. Once she watched me throw a five-pound note into the fire instead of the chocolate wrapper which was crammed inside my other pocket.

Nanna never altered. Her hair had always been supernaturally white, smoothly permed into snowy terraces. She dressed in suits – her 'costumes' – wool mixes in winter, polyester for the summer. Underneath she wore pastel blouses with floppy bow ties or a frill. She was dazzlingly clean, right down to her beige shoes from Clarke's – shoes so clean there was barely a mark on the soles. Nanna was what the ads would call not just clean but deep down clean. She didn't speak often, preferring to communicate by a sniff or a tissue dabbed at the corners of her mouth.

The closer I came to home, the more sharply I could picture her clenched and watchful face. One Christmas I couldn't take it any longer. I turned back.

When Jack realised what was happening he made me pull in.

'Ring up for me. Tell them I'm feeling unwell.'

'You'd only have to go another time. It's not so bad once you get there. A couple of days, what does it matter?'

'I hate her,' I said. 'I wish she was dead.'

'No you don't.' He was shocked. 'Come on Katie, I'm not telling lies for you. If you feel that strongly you should talk it through.'

Like they would in Jack's family. His mother was a food stylist, his father a psychiatrist, his grandparents artists and academics. There, on the hard shoulder outside Knutsford, I started to dislike Jack almost as much as Nanna. He was her favourite anyway. She preferred men to women.

Jack took over the driving. Neither of us spoke for the rest of the way. If that Christmas had ended the way it began, we would never have seen the New Year in together, never eaten Whiskied Pheasant in his mother's country cottage. But when we arrived in Manchester we found the bad fairy had vanished. Stone was flesh and blood again, the frog a handsome prince. All the spells were broken because Nanna wasn't there.

'She's being funny,' said my mother.

Nanna had decided she couldn't manage in her semi. She'd seen her neighbour's daughter move into the house next door, converting the upper storey into a granny flat.

'There isn't room in this house,' my mother kept saying, 'I've got Frank to think of, and the boys. She must see that. She knows damn well.'

Frank had been married to my mother for years, but Nanna still spoke his name as an insult, biting hard on the first two letters and choking on the last. She saw him as some kind of white slaver, sending my mother out cleaning to support a stranger's brats. The boys themselves she more or less tolerated.

'You don't think she'd actually sit by herself in the attic all day? We'd be on top of one another. If she was to put the old place on the market, she could buy herself somewhere nice. A retirement flat. They're luxury apartments. I told her that. You've got your privacy, but if you do need any help – she agreed with me. She even took the brochures.'

'Soon blow over,' said Frank.

'It's not Christmas without Nanna.'

My mother had a point. One thing about Nanna, she took rituals very seriously, always wore her paper hat and insisted on reading the jokes from the crackers. Maybe there was another side to her somewhere.

A ripple of regret passed across my mother's face and then was gone. Frank squeezed her shoulder as he moved to top us up – no one here now to ask how much we'd drunk already. She looked soft and young, dressed in a loose shirt and jeans instead of the usual frumpy flowered dress. Frank had lost the frown that made his face all chin and eyebrows. They weren't so bad, either of them, for their age.

Jack, Nanna said when she was in a good mood, reminded her of my father. Dad was her ideal – smartly dressed and well spoken, a gentleman who still remembered to send flowers for her birthday. (Or his secretary did; I got the same bouquet on mine.) To think, my mother had packed him in for some chap who worked on the railways!

'You have to remember,' Mum said, 'Nanna grew up in a different time. There was no divorce then. If you were divorced there was a finger pointed at you. I couldn't tell Nanna you and Jack live together.'

With Nanna gone, Jack was allowed in with me. The costume dolls watched us undressing, their fat-cheeked faces like rows of identical pale plums. Jack, in his underpants, fiddled with the catch of a lacquered jewellery case. As he raised the lid, the opening bars of the Blue Danube waltz started to play painfully in funeral time. A tiny, toothpick-legged ballerina, mounted on the red velvet lining, quivered then stopped.

'Jack, no!' I called, pulling the sheets over my head. 'You'll break it!' I made myself a tent under the covers, lit pink by the bedroom light. Warmed by my own body heat, I used to hibernate for hours when I was small. But now there was some one to play with. Jack had climbed over the spare mattress, and was trying to push me out. 'Jack, stop it! Shush!' We smothered our giggles. But I didn't really care. Who was there to tell us off?

A knock on the door. 'Katie?' my mother whispered. 'Katie?'

We froze. I was hanging over the edge of the bed with my head brushing the carpet. I could see the back issues of *Smash Hits* stacked under the bed.

'Katie?' she said. 'It's snowing. Look out of the window.'

Nanna made her peace with us, eventually. Then, after a bad fall at Easter, she decided to move into sheltered housing. But she was cheerful, Mum said. She was thriving. She'd even bought Frank a present for helping her move – a silver cigarette lighter. She probably hadn't noticed he gave up three years ago.

I saw her for myself at the Spring Bank Holiday. We were having the worst May on record. I almost didn't drive because of the floods. Jack and I were in France for the summer, then at half term I found some excuse. This time Jack didn't try to change my mind. We'd set a date, finally – April next year – and he was saving all his arguments for the wedding plans.

In December, I packed pyjamas and a hot water bottle, certain of Nanna in her chair by the Christmas tree, the grisly spirit of years past, present and yet to come. Last year would never be repeated. It was a secret place we could never find again. How often is there really a genuine white Christmas? It was more like a holiday than going home.

But Nanna wasn't back in place. She wasn't arriving on Christmas Eve and going back after Boxing Day. She wasn't even eating Christmas dinner with us. I didn't have to see her at all, if I didn't want to. Mum was popping round, she said, early on Boxing Day morning. If I wanted a lie-in she could take my present for me. I was so relieved I didn't ask any questions.

I was drinking gin and tonic, with the dog laid over my lap, scarcely seeming to breathe. He was getting on, poor sod; I poked him gently to check he was alive. I could feel the distant thud of rap from Adam's room. My other stepbrother, Paul, was down the pub. Frank was discussing United's progress with Jack. The TV spluttered now and then into a gunfire or a car chase. I was ready for bed, though it was only half past ten. All I needed was the strength to pull myself out of the armchair.

Then my mother spoke. She said, 'Never mind Katie, it'll grow back in time for the wedding.'

'What do you mean?'

'Makes you look like a lad.'

I touched the bare nape of my neck, gone suddenly cold. 'Jack likes my hair short.'

'So what? He's being nice to you. How much did that set you back, dare I ask? Should have gone to the barber's for short back and sides.'

It wasn't like my mother to criticise the way I looked. I could've passed a few comments about her own hair, badly coloured in piebald blonde and brown. Or the folly of pink lipgloss against an aging skin. Or the habit of biting her nails, piling up the little threads in a systematic heap on the arm of the chair. Her face was greenish in the tree lights. She looked almost evil.

That was when I realised something was wrong. I could see the difference suddenly and completely. Frank's jollity was a cover-up. He was pouring refills before we'd even taken our first sip, still going on about United's defence without stopping to draw breath. I never thought he was especially keen on football.

He was protecting my mother. What was he trying to hide? Was there trouble in their marriage? Was she ill? Perhaps one of them was going to lose their job, and they were keeping it a secret so as not to spoil Christmas.

Jack said I was dramatising. But he didn't know Frank and Mum like I did. He hadn't lived here. Small details had changed, things that might seem trivial to an outsider. We had a fake tree instead of a real one. Cups of tea tasted – not off, exactly, kind of stale. The house even smelt differently.

That night Jack and I were chaste as newborns. I couldn't get comfortable in the wobbly old bed, my cheek wedged against the anaglypta wall. I lay awake listening to the creaks and mutterings a house grown less familiar. I don't know what time Paul got back. I hadn't wound the old alarm clock – I hated the ticking – but the luminous dial read three when I heard the door bang, and somehow I believed that was the real time.

'Teenagers,' Jack said the next morning. 'Bet you were the same.'

But Adam hadn't come downstairs all Christmas Eve, not even to get a can out the fridge. The boys were in hiding. I knew. I just knew. It couldn't have been my fault, could it? Had I done something wrong?

In the morning, as we prepared the vegetables, Mum started on schoolteachers, how we have it dead easy, long holidays and overpaid – more Nanna's type of sermon than my mother talking to me

I tried changing the subject. Shouldn't I call round to Nanna's just for an hour? After all she hadn't seen me for six months. She might like to hear about the wedding.

'No, don't.' Mum slit the sprouts methodically, without looking at me.

'Why not?'

'It'll only upset you. I should've told you this before but she's not in the sheltered housing. She started to go funny. We had to put her in a home.'

'You're not to blame,' I told her.

'Did I say I was? Just one of those things, isn't it? Chemicals in the brain.'

'I should see her though.'

'What's the point? She won't know you.'

All those years I spent moaning about duty visits – and now I was being a good girl, my mother was stood in the way.

'You don't know what those places are like. I hope to God I never get to that stage. You've no idea Katie, young girl like you.'

That did it. 'Come on,' I said, 'how old do you think I am? I don't exactly lead a sheltered life. You should see what I have to cope with at school. I have to take some of those kids and wipe their faces before I can even start trying to teach. That's on the days when they turn up at all. Some of them never have a proper meal. They bring in four packets of crisps a day, two for break and two for dinner. If they're at school in time for break. Some of them don't leave home till their mum's out of bed, and they've been up until two in the morning watching telly. Then their dads come threatening me, asking why they can't read and write.'

'Okay,' she said, 'though I don't know what that's got to do with your Nanna. You can come if you're so keen. So long as you're ready for nine. I haven't got time to wait.'

It wasn't my fault. It was Nanna who was making everyone miserable. She had to spoil things even when she wasn't there. In fact, I might have preferred Christmas dinner with Nanna at the table. At least we would have made an attempt at conversation. Even Frank was quiet, staring into his plate like a hermit doing penance. Jack gabbled on about how good the turkey was when he knew very well the whole meal was overcooked. Just the way Nanna would have liked it – the boiled veg disintegrated, the roast potatoes mummified. I drank too much. The wine was as tasteless as the turkey, but unlike the turkey it slipped down my throat easily. I was in the grip of something stronger than my customary ennui. I was under anaesthetic. I dozed away most of the afternoon and spent Christmas night willing the clock to move forwards to bedtime. I was filling a hot water bottle on the stroke of eleven (Jack was still watching *Airplane*) when my mother came into the kitchen.

'Have I shown you this?' she said, plucking a typewritten letter from the wooden rack that Paul, or maybe Adam, made at school.

I read slowly, at first not understanding any of it. And then she explained. It dated back to September.

Dear Mrs. Cosgrove,

I am currently researching a book which deals in some depth with the famous 'Beauty and the Beast' murder trial of 1937. I have written several times to your mother, Mrs. Hilda Bracegirdle, in connection with this case, and even tried to visit her personally, but I am afraid that she is unwilling to speak to me. I should be most grateful if you could persuade her to change her mind. It is vital to my book that I talk to this key witness. I should take up very little of her time. Perhaps you yourself have some recollection of your mother talking about the case? If so, your memories would be most valuable.

Yours sincerely,
Ashley Spencer

Mum had never heard of the Beauty and the Beast case, but she'd been tickled to think of her mother on the fringes of a real life Agatha Christie. Nanna was vague when she mentioned the letter. 'Oh yes,' she said, 'that's the chap who keeps writing. I can't be doing with that. Not at my age. It's all in the past. Dead and buried.'

She could only have been six or seven at the time. Perhaps she saw something she'd sooner forget.

Spencer rang in the morning – half past eight the phone went – as soon as he'd received my mother's answer. She was just leaving for work.

He apologised for the intrusion, and what he had to say would, obviously, come as rather a shock. But she really ought to know that in fact Nanna was sixteen years old at the time of the case. In 1936 she was living in Sutton Coldfield under the name of Florence Pargeter.

This Florence Pargeter was a shy girl who worked in a corner shop, close by the church where she taught Sunday school. One Friday evening, her mother became concerned about Florence. It was nearly ten o'clock, and she still wasn't home from choir practise. The policeman asked if Florence might not have a boyfriend. Or gone dancing with some pals. 'Oh no,' said

Mrs. Pargeter, not my Florence, she's not the type. The policeman laughed. He said, you'd be surprised love. Not to worry. If she isn't back by morning then we'll have to think again.

Mrs. Pargeter knew her daughter. A minute late was as good as a week. They still hadn't found the madman who'd stabbed a young girl to death by the old quarry. The morning after Florence disappeared, the vicar's wife was found in the churchyard with her throat cut. By Thursday the police had dragged a female corpse from the canal.

Spencer's voice was so loud that my mother had to hold the earpiece at arm's length. At first his story was difficult to follow. Yet it seemed predictable, like a film she'd seen already. And by the time she spoke to me, she had it all pat like a child's bedtime story.

The body wasn't Florence. But Mrs. Pargeter was still convinced her girl was dead. Florence was all she had. Her husband had died of TB, and she herself was an invalid, scarcely able to leave the house. A week passed, then a month. Some startling news came.

The Reverend Theobald Crisp had been arrested leaving a casino on the French Riviera. He was accompanied by his valet – soon revealed as Florence with her hair cropped like a boy's.

'She wasn't wicked,' said my mother, 'just naïve.' She had no idea the vicar's wife was dead. He'd told her they had to disguise themselves in case she sent private detectives to steal back the family jewels – the jewels he had pawned after they arrived in Paris. Florence fell to her knees at the policemen's feet, begging them to believe in her lover's innocence. It was said she resembled Madeleine Carroll; her picture in the papers made a complete contrast to that of the squat, heavy-jowled Reverend. Inconsolable with grief, she was spared criminal charges on the condition that she testify for the prosecution.

'I've got it somewhere,' Mum told me, 'Mr. Spencer sent me a photocopy. "Beauty and the Beast".'

'And does it look like her?'

'These old photographs are all the same.'

The first rope they used on the Reverend snapped, holding up the execution for some time. He spoke tenderly of Florence, so they said, as he waited for the second knot to be tied. She was rumoured to be half way across the Atlantic, possibly under an alias, on her way towards a screen test. That was where Ashley Spencer picked up the trail.

Spencer was convinced that Florence had turned into Stella Knight, and then into Susan Bird, and finally into the Hilda Bird who married Arthur Bracegirdle in Manchester on July 7th, 1946. Spencer tracked her through Hollywood, Chicago and back to the Riviera, where she'd spent the summer before the war on the yacht of a certain Otis P. Johnson III. He was particularly anxious to shed light on her movements between 1940 and 1943, when she turned up as a secretary at Rolls Royce in Hulme.

'I had to laugh,' Mum said. 'Honestly Katie, can you see your Nanna running off to the States? We had enough of a struggle getting her on the coach to Llandudno. You'd never catch her going abroad. There's nobody on this earth as strait-laced as she is. Look at the way she brought me up. Half past ten on the dot I had to be home. And then it was where've you been, what you been up, who with. If I was ten seconds late she'd be waiting with the belt. I can't see her carrying on with a vicar, can you? Or dressed up as a boy.'

'Did it hurt?' I asked.

'What?'

'When she hit you with the belt.'

She shrugged. 'You get used to it.'

My mum told Spencer, politely, that he was mistaken. But she found herself wondering. In the years that she'd been a home help, the old people she worked with had always – wherever they came from, whatever they were like as individuals – been desperately keen to tell their life stories. Nanna never reminisced. She couldn't stand, she said, people harping on about the past.

Well that was Nanna for you. She just wasn't sentimental. If there were no sepia portraits on her sideboard that wasn't surprising because there were no other photographs either, just the porcelain figurines that Nanna collected. My mother had never known her grandparents on that side. She vaguely imagined they'd been killed in the war. Grandad, Mum's dad, had been one of thirteen, so there was never any shortage of relations. Nanna was quick to taken offence; if she had any brothers or sisters, she'd probably fallen out with them.

Mum didn't want to pester her too much over Spencer. Most likely there'd been a mix-up with some other Hilda Bracegirdle. But she thought she'd say something, just casually, the next time she fetched her over for Sunday dinner.

When she pressed Nanna's buzzer there was no reply. She wondered for a moment if Nanna had gone to wait in the car park. She was, after all, at least three minutes late. As soon as some one came out she slipped through the main entrance and found Nanna's door. Once again, no response. Hearing movement inside she knocked harder.

The fat woman across the hallway came out to watch. 'She won't answer,' she said, 'she won't answer for no one.'

The door opened just as my mother was trying to peer through the spyhole. She was face to face with an angry toothless hag, dressed in a nightie, who was demanding to know who the bloody hell she was.

'My stomach turned over,' Mum said. 'Course she knew who I was really, it didn't take her long. Once I'd opened all the curtains and got her washed and dressed she was back to her old self again. She hadn't wound up the clock, that was it. She'd lost track. You should have heard her moan about the beef – all dried up it was, by the time we got back here. Frank never thought to take it out of the oven.

'Next thing you know there's a phone call. Would I please see to my mother. She was walking around in her slip, banging at people's doors. They said they'd noticed it for a while, how she was getting more confused. But how would they know? She didn't mix much. She wasn't a sociable person. She wouldn't have gone to the whist drives and bingo, no chance. She was all there when I saw her, except for that one time. We all get confused now and then, don't we, doesn't mean you've gone senile.

'Anyway, we drove up there right away. You should have seen the state of that flat. I thought kids must have got in at first. As for Nanna – it broke my heart to see her like a child. You know what a pride Nanna took in herself. I've seen it happen before, usually if they've had a fall or something. But I never thought my mother'd go that way. She's too sharp. It frightens you, Kate. Makes you think of the future.

'Remember those figurines? They were worth a bit, you know. She told me once they were going to you. Not much left of them now. Remember the lady with the greyhound? There was just a little chip off its ear where I knocked it. I was only seven years old then. She went mad. I knew she would. I ran off and hid in your Grandad's shed. She found me straight away of course. Just a little chip.' She gave a sort of chuckling sigh. 'Six of the best, then straight to bed. That one's in pieces now. You can't stick them back together.'

The kettle had boiled half an hour ago. I stood leaning against the sink with my empty hot water bottle. She'd picked up a tea towel, as if she was just being distracted from what she meant to do. My mother never spoke to me like this before, as one friend confiding in another. I could see everything as clearly as my own memories – the fat woman's folded arms as she watched across the deep piled corridor; my mother knocking hesitantly at the door; the toothless crone in her winceyette nightie. I saw the pale and slippery porcelain ladies with their minute eyes and mouths and long, elegant hands, each holding a sheath of flowers, a pet or a musical instrument. Most of all, I saw Nanna's own dry white hand pulling open a kitchen drawer. I could see a man's belt coiled among the sellotape and string, the elastic bands and old paper bags neatly folded inside. I could see the child dragged screaming out of the potting shed.

'You never hit me,' I said.

'Oh, I must've smacked you now and then.' She started to dry the dishes. And then she began, as if delivering a speech: 'I'll never forget, when my dad lay there dying – she wouldn't let me in – made me feel like I was evil.'

Go on, I wanted to say. Go on, tell me.

'All because of Frank. We weren't hurting anyone.'

Go on, go on. 'Shall I make a cup of tea?'

She shook her head as she arranged the mugs carefully on the their hooks by the cereals shelf, making sure that every one was facing in the right direction. I thought there were tears in her eyes.

'When we came to move her into that place, I looked into her papers. There were no letters, certificates, nothing. All I want is peace of mind, that's all, to know for sure.'

Frank came in, raised the kettle and flicked the switch. 'We never will,' he said.

'Mr. Spencer sent us a Christmas card. Apparently there's going to be something on the telly. He's even asked us to be in it.'

'No chance,' Frank told me.

I was disappointed.

'Bad enough as it is,' Mum went on. 'People pointing a finger.'

'Supposing they do, how long till it's blown over? You know what it's like, everyone's going on about some programme, then next week they've moved on to something different.' Frank turned to me. 'Tell your mother, she's too sensitive.'

'I can still get through to her,' Mum said. 'She knows me. I think she'd find a way to tell me. If there was anything to tell.'

'Let it go.' Frank poured the water into the teapot with one smooth, decisive sweep. 'You're only torturing yourself.'

'You think it's true,' she snapped.

'The man's got the evidence. Don't take it so much to heart. It's nothing to be ashamed of. She was never accused of anything, was she? She was a victim herself, in a manner of speaking.'

I joined in. 'Was she in any danger, do you think? If he'd killed all those girls...'

'That wasn't him,' Frank said. 'It was only the wife he did in. Not the others.'

'So I don't understand,' I said, 'how did the body in the canal fit in with all this?'

My mother almost screamed. 'You make me sick! The way you stand there chatting like it was – I don't know – Inspector Morse – what if it was my name being dragged through the mud?'

I felt so sorry for her, I tried to take her in my arms. Very briefly, I felt the shock of contact, her body yielding to mine like a child's. Then she pulled away to drape the tea towel on the radiator. She was talking to Frank now about his turn to walk the dog. I was a mere spectator.

I had to tell Jack. He thought I was joking at first. 'Sounds like it's some kind of mix-up,' he said.

But I didn't doubt, for one minute, that Nanna really had been Florence Pargeter, Stella Knight or Susan Bird. Lying awake in the darkness, I could picture Florence, in her boyish disguise, as graceful as a Shakespearean heroine; and Stella, a moonlit figure smoking languidly by the rail of a great ocean liner; and Susan's wrist weighed down with diamonds that chinked like ice against her cocktail glass. I could almost see their faces, but I could only begin to imagine their lives.

My mother had warned me not to ask questions, though I couldn't see what difference it made if Nanna was gaga anyway. I had a feeling she might tell me things she wouldn't let my mother know. I was younger, more broad-minded, closer to the self that she'd suppressed for all these years.

Afterwards, Mum swore she'd kept her promise, to give me a knock at eight thirty. But by the time I woke up she'd already left. I had to wait till Frank had come back from walking the dog before I could ask him how to find Laburnum Lodge. Jack wanted to come with me. No, I said, this was women's business.

I just missed my mum, according to the office. 'Hilda's still in the lounge, I expect.'

Fancy anyone daring to call Nanna by her Christian name.

'We haven't seen you before, have we? Perhaps you'd like a look around. We try to keep their minds alert. We run craft and music-making groups. Hilda loves a sing-along. And the reminiscence project – have you seen our little booklet?'

The matron passed me a stapled pamphlet, with the words DAYS GONE BY printed on the cover.

'Quite a character is Hilda.'

The lounge was the size of a ballroom, done up with flouncy curtains and cheap candelabra, whose bulbs were lit despite the winter sunshine. Metallic Christmas chains criss-crossed the ceiling. The harshness of the light, and the very size of the room, made it difficult to focus on the old folk ranged around the walls or in rows facing a noisy, wall-mounted television. I'd expected to spot Nanna straight away but now I wondered how much she might have changed. I felt suffocated by the heat and the smell of cauliflower. I should never have come.

I peered into the wrinkled faces. Many were asleep, heads

dropped and dribbling or bent backwards, mouths wide open. Others watched me expectantly as I walked past, clutching the shop-wrapped present. A woman in the corner crooked her finger like a witch. 'You! Get over here!' Could that be Nanna? Her face without teeth was like a clenched fist. The white scraps of hair could have been Nanna's. Close to I saw the difference, but it was too late. The witch pulled me to her, cackling. 'Don't go, don't go.' She was so strong, I couldn't break her grip. 'No, I'm sorry,' I said. Her eyes were pitiful, as deep and clear as a six year old's.

'What you got for me? Give it!' She eyed the wrapping paper, desperately wanting to grab but not daring to let go of me. 'Cunt!' she shrieked. 'You fucking dirty bitch!' She bit me, or tried to, gums chewing at my hand.

I know how to stay calm. I've faced that same bottomless need in a child – oh please Miss, let me go home with you, please – but small children don't have the physical strength. The gums worked on my flesh like a suckling wolf. I wanted to rip her off me. I made Jack laugh when I told him she reminded me of the face huggers in *Alien*. But it wasn't funny at the time. It was repulsive.

The cadaverous man sitting stiffly in a straight-backed chair laid his paper on his lap. 'She shouldn't be in here. They should have places for people like that.' I could see parsnip-coloured ankles between his socks and trousers. 'Nurse! Nurse!'

A pale teenager in uniform appeared. 'You being a naughty girl, Mary?'

Mary gummed a naughty smile, and let me go.

'Hilda Bracegirdle?' said the teenager. 'She's over there.'

Asleep, in a corner. I should have seen her instantly,

because she hadn't changed at all. Her hair was still styled in the same rigid perm. Her paper white hands, with the plain gold band and the diamond solitaire, lay stiffly arranged on the arms of the tall, red vinyl chair. A travelling rug was wrapped round her knees. Half a dozen Mills and Boon were stacked neatly on the carpet. She couldn't be that bad if she was still reading hospital romances.

I sat on the red vinyl footstool, flicking through the booklet while I waited for her to wake up. I glanced at a page on working at the mill, then another about pawnshops, but I was looking for something more than these everyday routines.

The old lady next to Nanna spoke to me. 'Are you looking at our book? I'm in there, you know. So's Hilda. Have you come to see Hilda? Look, there she is.'

She leaned over to tap the page.

Hilda: I saw the Queen when she came to open the library – the old queen. I was at the back but I didn't half clap. I went with my mother. We took sandwiches.

'Mildred brought her tape recorder in, and then she typed it up for us. Isn't she clever?'

I sped through the other names, the Roses and Edies, the Harrys and Bills, and yes, the Florences. Some had lent pictures of their younger selves, photocopied into dark blots with empty white eyes. There were, of course, no pictures, of Nanna. But a voice labelled Hilda faded in and out of the chorus.

Hilda: I loved the Whit Walks. Protestants on Monday, Catholics Friday. You should have seen the Madonna. The Italians had the Madonna. If it rained on Friday we used to say, God knows his own.

Mildred: What did you wear for the Walks?

Doris: My sister made all my dresses.

'We didn't have much,' Nanna's neighbour told me, 'but we were satisfied.'

The chapters were headed *Childhood, Work, Family Life, War.* Perhaps that really did cover every experience. Looking into Nanna's sleeping face, I could see nothing of Florence, taking the scissors to her tumbling locks; nothing of Stella gazing into the dark waters.

'Sleeping Beauty!' said the old lady. 'You should wake her up, you know. Give her a nudge. She won't mind. We let ourselves nod off because there's nothing else to do.'

Nanna smiled at me foolishly. But it was unlike her smile; the mouth curled instead of clenching. When she spoke my name – 'Katie!' – she seemed to melt with delight. She looked as cuddly as a Disney granny.

The old lady in the next chair touched my hand. 'Thinks you're her sister,' she whispered. 'She thinks she's sixteen.'

Instead of her two piece costume, Nanna was dressed in a navy blue polyester frock with a white palm tree on the front. Her expression became more cautious as she scanned me.

'You've had an Eton crop,' she said. 'Wait till Dad sees it, our Katie! He'll take the belt to you!'

I didn't know what was best, to play along or set her straight, so I wished her a happy Christmas and passed her the present. She ripped the paper off, grumbled over the cellophane, and finally pushed a whole chocolate into her mouth. 'Want one?' she asked sweetly, then snatched them back before I had the chance. They were half-melted anyway, in the fetid atmosphere.

Her mouth was smeared with chocolate. She seemed to

have forgotten I was there. She was concentrating on whatever was on telly, some Arabian Nights adventure in the stained glass blues and reds of early Technicolor. The visit was over. But it seemed rude to leave it at that – rude, not to Nanna, but to the woman in the next chair and the cadaverous old man and the other residents who were watching the pair of us instead of the Boxing Day film.

'I was looking at your book. About the old days in Manchester.'

Ashley Spencer said you were Florence Pargeter from Sutton Coldfield.

'No washing machines in them days,' she said briskly.

Her neighbour nodded. 'The old mangle,' she said. 'And the dolly. Bet you don't know what that is.'

Ashley Spencer said you were an adulteress, an adventurer, the mistress of dubious men.

Nanna spoke through her second mouthful. 'Rag rugs on the floor.' Her fingers rooted blindly through the layers. 'Donkey stones.'

'Blackleading the grate.'

'You could leave your back door open. Not like now.'

'I remember I had this little dog. It was the Christmas Eve when they dropped the bombs on Manchester...'

'Shut up you old cow,' said Nanna. 'Who's talking to you?' Bits of chocolate were stuck to the front of her dress. She turned to me. 'What else have you got for me?'

'Mum was here this morning, wasn't she?' I said lamely.

'Who?'

'Mum.'

'My mother's dead.'

We sat in silence while the genii, the princess and the little boy in the turban flew their magic carpet into the turquoise sky. I was planning to vanish myself, when the girl in uniform came round. 'Dinner's in a minute, Hilda.' It was round about half past eleven. 'Have you been to the toilet?'

'I can't go on my own.'

'Yes you can.'

'I can't. I'll wet myself.' Nanna flinched as her face and fingers were rubbed clean with kitchen towel.

'No you won't. Take no notice,' the girl said, speaking to me. 'Don't you try taking her. She's only playing games. She can get about alright. She's a lot better off than some of these poor souls.'

'I'll wee my pants!' cried Nanna. 'I can't manage! I'm too old! Do you know how old I am? Go on, guess!'

Florence Pargeter, born 1920, Sutton Coldfield; Hilda Bracegirdle, born 1930, Manchester – what difference did it make? She was simply an old woman. She wasn't even Nanna any more.

'I'd better go,' I said, 'if you're having your lunch.'

I tidied the torn paper away, and picked up my coat. If I didn't get out of there soon I might faint with the heat.

Nanna's travel blanket dropped to the floor as she struggled to her feet. When I tried to help, she pulled away, balancing herself on a Zimmer frame. A chilly reptilian hand rested briefly on mine. 'Stupid old hag,' she muttered, 'strong as a horse, who'd have thought it? Silly bugger drops the knife. What's the matter, can't you take the sight of blood?'

'What do you mean, Nanna, what you talking about?'

'Here, let me do it.'

She moved the hand away, and started her steady progression towards the dining room. She heaved the Zimmer frame before her, lifting and smiting with surprising force. She seemed so small, hunched over the frame like an energetic snail.

'Florence!' I called after her. She didn't look back. She had left a damp patch on the seat of her chair.

I offered the last Belgian chocolate to the old lady. 'That's my name,' she said. 'I didn't know Hilda was a Florence as well. I never knew my husband was a Herbert till we signed the marriage license. He didn't like being Herbert, always called himself Jim. I'll save this for later, thankyou very much.' She wrapped the sticky chocolate in a tissue, and put it carefully inside her big brown handbag. 'I shan't be going into dinner. My son's coming for me. His wife's a beautiful cook. She's a lovely girl, do anything for you. Are you Hilda's grandchild? Thought so. I can tell. You've got her eyes.'

Jack laughed when I told him that bit: 'Beauty and the Beast!' My mother promised to find me the clipping Spencer sent her, with Florence's photo, but of course she never did. And I didn't tell her everything about my visit to Nanna. Those few muttered words seemed more and more insubstantial. I might not have even heard them properly. I might have imagined the almost wink, the hint of a Midlands accent.

Nanna had a stroke three weeks before the wedding. Now she can't communicate at all. As for Mum, she never speaks about the past. I rang her up just after the TV programme with its talk of new evidence and witnesses from the death cell. Frank wanted to sue, but she said it wasn't worth it. As time goes by, I think less about Florence and Stella and Susan, and more about

Jane Bracegirdle who became Jane Wallace and finally Jane Cosgrove. I think about the belt coiled inside the kitchen drawer. I imagine my mother holding her hand out for six of the best. I picture her knocking at Nanna's front door, while I'm waiting round the corner in the back of Frank's old van. I'm a child, not interested in why my mother's been crying. The grown up world is closed to me. All I care about is whether she'll buy me just an ordinary cornet or a ninety-nine.

She made me feel evil – all because of Frank – we weren't hurting anyone.

How angry my mother must have been when she first read Spencer's letter. But what kind of anger was it? I should like to know one day.

One thing did change after that Christmas. As soon as we got back home, Jack and I went looking for a sofa bed in the sales. Why did we always visit our families? There was no reason why they couldn't stay with us.

By the following Christmas, we'd moved from the flat to a house with a yard. Mum and Frank slept on the sofa bed, while the boys were squashed into what would be the baby's room.

'I don't feel like a Grandma,' said Mum. She didn't look like one either. She was her old self again. She'd stopped that systematic stripping of her nails, and she'd had her hair more subtly coloured and cut shorter. She loved the house, though she was a little peeved that I wouldn't take any of Nanna's old stuff, not even her surviving figurines.

'So what do you want the baby to call you?' Jack asked her.

'Oh that doesn't matter.'

'Granny,' said Frank.

My mum winced. 'Well, Nanna,' she said, 'it's always been

Nanna in our family.'

I said, 'What's wrong with your own name? Why not just Jane?'

'Not very respectful is it, Katie? What're you going to call the baby? That's what you should be thinking.'

Secretly, I made up my mind. Whoever she was, there was only one Nanna. My child would call my mother by her name. And if she was a girl, I could maybe call her Stella.

MAKING IT HAPPEN

His new car's a woman. He speaks to her softly, calling her baby, there, he says, there, come on now, you can do it, teasing the switches – lets try swapping these – setting to work with a tiny screwdriver. His hands work swiftly and gently. You can trust this man. He knows what he's doing.

'Once,' I tell him, 'I came off my bike in the hills round your way. I was lying on the road, then this car stopped and some one said, "It's alright, I'm a Swiss doctor…'

But he's not listening. He's far away from me now. I sit quietly holding a torch, watching his fingers tweak the wires, until the lights flick on, and we're flying into the city, past the skewed paint tin handle of the Hulme archway, towards the mercury glow of the Bridgewater Hall. MANCHESTER, the billboard says, MAKING IT HAPPEN.

'You don't drive?' he says. 'Never wanted to drive?'

Something clunks in the hull of the big Scimitar. The dials glow like moons on the dashboard. It's a clear March night; you can see the comet on its way round the universe. We know tonight is our beginning; we've passed through that secret door where something is agreed. He sends me a quick fractured glance, and then he keeps his eyes steady on the road ahead.

My little brother David is thirty years old. Birthday cards and wrapping paper litter the long work surfaces, newly installed by his father-in-law. Orange and lime couples are admiring the orange and blue kitchen, stroking the streamlined wood, discovering the fridge behind a panelled door, releasing tiered spice racks hidden in a corner. Still wearing my black winter best, I flit like a fly between the little splinter groups.

These are people I only ever see on David's birthday. I find out their names, and how they fit together, and then I've forgotten them all by next year.

No mistaking Sophie and David for anything but the two halves of a pair. Masculine and blonde, they could represent Progress. They could be carved in bronze outside the town hall. They've been together forever, for as long as I've been alone.

Sophie asks me brightly, am I seeing anyone?

'Yes, yes I am actually.'

She's startled, leans forward to hear more; but as I speak, I'm scared that I'm unravelling my fortune. Untangled from my tongue, the story's going to snap and vanish. When I imagine this man, I can't remember what he looks like. Yet his light, cautious voice keeps running through my head like my own memory. This is a dangerous state in which to find yourself. It is not entirely safe.

'Is he nice? How old is he? What's his name?'

I can't tell anyone, especially not Sophie. There is a particular reason.

'Go on, you can tell me. Is it anyone I know?'

I'm blushing girlishly. People keep shoving between us to get to the beers in the fridge. Everybody's still in the kitchen, no one's moved into the lime-coloured living room. Just one or two are drifting out the back door for a smoke.

'Well, whatever, I'm very pleased for you,' Sophie says in her clear, formal voice. 'It's about time.' I like my sister-in-law, but I've never really got to know her. She scares me a little. I'd like to ask her to put on eyeliner that way, flicked boldly across the lids like Japanese calligraphy. My hand's never steady enough for much more than a pencil smudge.

Suddenly she turns solemn, gazing at her wine glass, then glancing swiftly into my eyes. 'Things haven't been going so well between David and me. In fact I'm leaving him. It's alright, I've got somewhere to go. I'm moving out at Easter. He doesn't know that yet.'

'I can't believe what I'm hearing. It's as if the wrong sound-track's been dubbed onto her lips. Maybe she's joking. But her face is set hard.

'Has David said anything?'

'He told me he was going to start a family.'

She laughs bitterly. 'How can we have children? We hardly see each other. He sets the alarm for five-thirty. I don't get home till eight. But that's not it, it's not just that. We never talk. David won't talk. He can't talk.'

This is delusion, madness. Music leaks in from the lime-green room, the Chemical Brothers, fierce and insistent, but still nobody's moving. David's passing round the garlic bread. He asks Sophie, should he get the potatoes out or leave them for later.

'Anyway,' she repeats, looking for paper towels. I'm happy for you. Where is he tonight?'

At a dinner party. One of his old-fashioned words, 'dinner party' like 'going dutch', like 'cinema'. He calls my cunt a fanny; he's changed a daughter's nappy, you can tell. I can see his friends, landscaped dimly round a weathered table. What does he say when they ask what he's been doing?

Maybe now, at the mid-point of David's party, which coincides with the closing stages of a Saturday meal, as the ice cream puddles in the dishes and the smell of coffee rises like incense, some one might say come on, haven't seen you for ages. He's sly and self-satisfied, searching himself for his packet of grass. 'I've been busy.' He starts talking about the car, how he waited a few days before putting in an offer. If it was gone, too bad. Serendipity. But a man of fifty needs to drive a Scimitar.

Every morning my brother cycles towards the university at dawn, numbers already whirring through his brain. Hunched across the handlebars, he scents the fizzing blossom, the season on the turn. But most of his mind is slotted into the disk drive, running beyond the blue morning towards infinity. If you ask what he's doing, he'll try to explain; but he really can't go beyond surface politeness. What David does can't be translated into ordinary speech.

If those two break up, there's no hope for anyone. I remember asking him at his wedding, what it felt like to be married. He just laughed. Then suddenly he said, 'You know what it's like when you first meet some one? It's a light going on. Everything's clear.'

No, I didn't understand what he meant, not from real life. From songs, maybe, or the movies – the cinema – but that's just pretend, you can't take it seriously. He was as clumsy as a farmer's boy in his wedding suit. Sophie looked immaculate, larger than life in her glowing white dress.

Right now, my brother's in the lime-green room skimming through his old vinyl. Small candles have been lit along the scrubbed wooden shelves, and glass vases filled with gerbera, as bright and as perfectly round as lollipops. He smiles happily across the empty room. 'Thirty, eh? Over the hill.' He swigs orange juice; David has no vices. He plucks out a record – seventies funk that played at the clubs, already nostalgic, when

I was a student. He braces himself for the music and, as we flip into the synthetic beat, he moves with the considered grace of a big man, holding himself like a skater on the stripped and polished floor. Gradually the room fills, and like the song says, these are good times tonight. When you're dancing, you're part of the crowd and you're also by yourself. You're here and somewhere else at the same time. A woman my age needs to do this now and then.

I've lain awake since dawn, watching the bow of his back, listening to his breathing, waiting to meet him again in the flesh. We're not young, but we're new to each other, our bodies freshly minted in the light of day.

He says, 'You didn't come – did you?'

'Don't let it bother you.'

'It didn't.'

I pull at his thick grey hair. He chuckles. 'Men are beasts.' Almost unconsciously, he rolls a cigarette. 'Of course the female orgasm's less intense than the male. The woman lasts longer, she reaches a kind of plateau, but physiologically, the muscular reaction, the blood pressure and so on, register more strongly in the male.'

I love it when he talks this crap. I love watching his guarded, smuggler's face – the knuckled cheekbones, the secret strain around the eyes. I like to witness the controlled assembly of the tin, the papers, the green bag of Golden Virginia, the constant relighting of squashed cigarettes.

'Well you know,' I tell him, 'the best sex is purely mechanical. Some one you're never going to have to see again.'

'You haven't told me about the party,' he says abruptly.

'Did you mention me to Sophie?'

'She told me she was leaving David.'

'What, and let him keep the kitchen?'

'She's not joking, she's got it all planned.'

'That's just Sophie being dramatic.'

'She's not going to you is she?'

'Lord no. She wouldn't set foot in my hovel.'

As he ditches the fag end and glances towards me, something in his face suddenly shifts. For a moment, I catch Sophie's fractured gaze. Physically, the two of them couldn't be more different – the ageing bandit, the healthy young goddess. Yet some phantom presence, beyond skin and bone, turns one into the other like those pictures that switch between a rabbit and a duck. Go on, said Sophie, you can tell me, is he nice?

'I worked bloody hard on that kitchen.'

We shuffle limbs, our bodies still not accustomed to each other. He starts to work at me again, stroking my cunt – my fanny – with calm, circular movements. Is that nice, he asks me, is it good? I can feel myself crumbling, yet something remains, something hard and metallic, bolting my cunt to my brain. Useless. Still here. This is such a drag for him.

He changes angles, he's determined, but it won't do any good. Because I'm starting to love him already, and because I'm afraid of such longing, because you can't take what you want, how can you, you find what you've lost only when it's been forgotten. Because I'm thinking all these things right now, listening to the tidal rush of the motorway traffic, wondering what time it is, wishing he'd just leave.

He says, 'What's the matter babe, what is it?' I cover my eyes with my elbow. I can't bear to meet his gaze. But then something lifts. I can't stop myself. I'm there, alone, somewhere with him, I'm there.

'You don't remember me,' he said, 'I'm Sophie's dad. We met at the wedding.' And yes, I remembered, faintly. He didn't give her away. He refused, or maybe he'd not been allowed. There was some sort of danger around Sophie's father. He was a solitary, gypsyish figure, rolling a fag on his way out of church.

My own mum and dad were still together then. That wedding cake was the last one he made. Mum was working at the wool shop. David had just finished his thesis.

As for me, my history's a blank. I was being very good; I know that. I held myself stiff and upright, in high heels that stuck in the damp turf. Everyone was a little under-dressed, in optimistic spring fashions. But at least the rain held off. We can't complain. Sophie's such a lovely girl, you must be proud of David, I hear he's very clever. I smiled and nodded, knowing what those aunts and cousins were dying to talk about once my back was turned. I couldn't hold down anything in those days. I lost my job. I left my key in my front door and had everything stolen. Not everyone knew the latest, but there was enough to be going on with.

As we gathered for the photographer, a gust of wind blew the blossom from the trees, like feathers bursting from a pillow. Sophie's mother went hurtling after her hat. She had very short, colourless hair, almost shaven – my mum said she looked like she'd been to the nit nurse – and dangly earrings that swung madly when she laughed. Her bloke was a shaggy red-bearded lawyer based somewhere in Moss Side. Posing with them, Sophie looked like a swan between two parrots.

Well, her father told me, watching bride and groom kiss on camera, those two ought to be happy, a Pisces and a Virgo. I said, you don't believe that shit, do you really think the planets move around us? I felt a sudden rush in my veins, as sharp as vodka. I wanted an argument but I knew I had to control myself, so I covered up with some only-joking pleasantry and moved out of his orbit as quickly as I could.

Sophie's parents were old hippies. That explained her lacquered gloss, the job in hotel management, the hired cars and the bridesmaids crowned with rosebuds. Her mother ran rebirthing sessions. Her father sold books round the markets but, so far as I could tell, he mostly survived doing odd jobs for people. Sophie was smarter than either. She saw the conventions but she also knew how to use them.

I must have already stopped drinking by then, because later I remember him pouring out champagne, and me covering the clean glass with my hand, and him teasing me, don't you have any vices…My hand slipped, I misjudged the distance, and the glass rolled on its side. Thank God it didn't fall. Sophie was watching us; so was my mother.

Mum had warned me: don't make an exhibition. That was all; we both knew what she meant. Dad had discreetly left the room to check the oven. I could smell the greaseproof paper singeing. The cake would be ready when it was nearly burnt, the sultanas popping and crisp on the surface. I used to go into work with Dad on Saturdays, long before David was born. The bakery ovens were set deep in the wall, like in 'Hansel and Grettel'. I'd watch him push the trays inside the endless darkness. His blue tattoo glowed like a gas flame through the swirling fair hairs on his arm. A big shy man, like David; whereas I feature my mother. That must have been when he visited the other woman – on Sundays, after he stopped taking me with him. It was going on for years apparently. She was an old flame; they'd been at school together.

I threw a brick through my ex-husband's windscreen. At least, I thought it was his until I saw another red Capri parked opposite. It was in the *South Manchester Express*, just an inch or so. But Sophie's dad might not have known that, any more than I knew the disgrace that made him a ghost at the nuptials. You can't read history in a face. You can't predict the future either.

The truth is, we didn't really meet at David's wedding. I was hardly there at all. Nor did I really see him the second time, on a train somewhere between Todmorden and Littleborough. I was rummaging through my backpack, hauling out the cagoule, the mineral water, the map and the books, but not my ticket nor my purse. They'd disappeared. I spoke calmly to the guard. I said, 'I'm sorry, I don't know what to do' – and then a muffled voice was offering to pay. I sensed a blurred figure standing next to me, by the shipshape wooden ladder they keep on local trains. I thought how kind strangers are sometimes. But mostly I was thinking about my money gone, and my bank cards, and everything dropping away from me.

I have been my good self for a very long time. I work hard. I keep myself clean. My doors are locked tight, and if I take a drink it's only one glass before bedtime. I am not the woman I was at the wedding. But still he said, with some surprise, 'Have you taken up cycling?' Sophie's dad. The jack of all trades, the odd job man who believed in destiny.

The purse was in a side pocket all along. I found it right

after I'd cancelled my cards, just as if some spiteful fairies had swiped it. Even then I couldn't guess which way the dice were rolling. I forgot that I'd promised to pay him back. *'De nada,'* he said, 'you can buy me a drink next time there's a wedding. 'No,' I insisted, 'I can't be beholden.' *Beholden,* one of my mother's expressions, like *showing yourself up,* like *exhibition,* like *taking a pride in yourself.*

I forgot all about Sophie's dad.

If his van hadn't been nicked, he wouldn't have been on the train at all; if Sophie hadn't nagged him to finish the van in time for David's party. Don't worry, he said, it'll sort itself out. You can pick up a van anywhere. It was just that in the meantime he'd spotted this old Scimitar, the sort of car a man deserved before he was too clapped out to enjoy it.

They were paying him good money, David told me. But he liked to do everything in his own time. He hated being rushed. It was then I remembered the number on the ticket – one night when the flat seemed especially empty, when I'd showered and packed for work, and there was nothing else to do but wait for Monday. Was that a five or a three? If I chose the wrong number, I'd leave it. As I dialled I realised he hadn't told me his name. But I recognised his voice the moment he answered, almost as if we'd been lifelong friends.

And so, when David calls my mind's tuned to some one else, who often calls me these days, just as the sun goes down, carrying the phone with him as he clanks around an invisible kitchen, searching out his baccy, making a brew, the radio rattling on in the background.

'I was thinking about your boiler,' says David, in his usual tentative manner.

The boiler? That's a winter's tale, old history, no sooner said than mended. Yet I write down the number he gives me, and even repeat it even though I know every digit by heart.

'Actually it's Sophie's dad. He could fix it for you when he comes to do our bathroom.'

'How is Sophie?'

'Fine, she's fine.' Now my mind is firmly back here in Manchester, I can sense a weight on the line. 'She's working over Easter. Some big conference.'

'So what are you up to?'

'Oh you know, this and that. Want to come for a bike ride tomorrow?'

'I can't. What about Monday?'

'I don't know, I've stuff to do for work. And I'm supposed to get the bathroom ready...'

'Is everything alright?'

'What do you mean?'

'Are things okay between you?'

He laughs nervously. 'Why shouldn't they be?'

I wait to see if he'll go on; there's no pushing David. Outside, an ice cream van's playing a desperate version of 'Anchor's Away'. Spring has arrived. The clocks are going forward this weekend.

'Look,' says David, 'I'll ring you Sunday morning; I'm probably going to Mum's.'

Everything's fine. One day turns into another, running on paint rollers, disk drives, bicycle chains. But still Sophie could be gone for good. For all I know, David's sitting by himself in a half-empty house, the CDs divided, the gerbera wilted in the shiny glass vases. I'm hoping to be somewhere else on Sunday morning. But Sunday can wait.

The sun hasn't quite gone down on this Good Friday. The horizon's lemon-tinted, beneath a deepening violet blue. In the Manchester flatlands, the broad skies are our landscape, never the same from one day to the next. When it's dark, I'll look for the comet, a milky smudge towards the west.

To the east, three-quarters of an hour away, two hours by public transport, a man's still working on his car. Grit's caught in his teeth. His fingers are engraved with oil. He lives in a stone ruin at the top of a track – the sort of place a postman avoids, so he tells me, the sort of place where there might be rottweilers. The rain collects in oil cans and plastic bottles. The windows are boarded, the walls unplastered, the bare floors cluttered with builder's junk and the boxes of unsold books that he couldn't bear to part with. But there is a bed and a fire. You must take me as you find me, so he says.

She's beautiful, his ageing folly, his great blue streamlined boat, the Scimitar – more trouble than he thought, but he knows what he's doing. He settles into the driver's seat, relishing the spaciousness, then turns the key in the ignition. A cough, silence. He turns it again, come on baby, still she won't bite – for me, baby, please, just for me. He sighs, sits back, thinking almost nothing. Then he smokes a cigarette until it's time to try again.

NO PROBLEMO

No, not the cinema, not with the state his head's in today. And not swimming, think of Max getting dressed and undressed, doing buttons one by one, no thanks. Too wet for the park. So McDonald's it is. Max orders a Big Mac with small fries and a medium size root beer. Bill has a coffee in a polystyrene cup, too hot to drink, so he watches Max eroding the borders of his burger, tucking slips of lettuce back inside the bun.

'Nice is it?' Bill enquires. 'You enjoying that?' They could be father and son, a family portrait framed in the innumerable mirrors. 'Art Deco, I suppose,' he says, taking in the polished surfaces, the potted palms, the metallic prints of cars and ocean liners. 'You ever been to New York? Empire State Building, fourteen hundred and seventy two feet. It's not the tallest building now, but it's still impressive.'

'It's not as tall as Mount Everest,' says Max, fishing skinny fries from the carton. 'Maybe not,' says Bill struggling to remember just how high Everest is, in feet or is that metres? He's not sure if Max is precocious or small for his age. He's asked Bridget how old he is at several points in their relationship, and each time he's forgotten. The boys' eyes are hidden underneath his Dallas Cowboys hat. They've talked about the Dallas Cowboys before, and the difference between American and English football. Bill has been to Texas – not Dallas itself, but to Houston, a thousand miles away. Texas is three times bigger than Britain. Just imagine.

Max is wondering to himself, if Bill's here now in the afternoon does that mean he's going out tonight with Bridget? If so, will Rachel be his babysitter? Will she bring *Terminator 2*?

She said she would – next time if you go straight up to bed now and don't come down, and you don't tell your mum, you hear me? You don't tell her anything.

Max is the only person, the only one in his class, who hasn't seen the Terminator films. Except for Caspian, who doesn't even have a telly, whose family never wear shoes or have their hair cut, who can't eat anything but goat's milk and lentils. But Bridget won't listen. 'It's the violence,' she says, 'I won't have violence in my house. I don't want to know, Max, that's final.' Treating Max like a baby. But he isn't a baby. And he is not Caspian. He's the kind of kid who ought to see *Terminator 2*.

The coffee strips a layer from Bill's tongue. He suddenly feels ravenous, like some one who's never eaten. Max lifts the root beer briefly to his mouth, then takes another nibble from the brick-coloured bun. Nothing wrong with his appetite – he's just a slow eater. At Bridget's, they sit silently at either side of the table, watching him ponder his food. When Bill was a child, he ate separately, except on Sundays. He was brought up by his grandparents, amongst dark, Victorian heirlooms. Once he'd cleared his plate, he'd ask, please may I leave the table? *May I?* If he said 'can', he'd have to sit still until he remembered.

'So Mummy's having her hair done.'

'Viv's cutting it.'

The burger's much smaller now, chiselled into a rough octagon. Most of the other customers appear to be Chinese. Why should that be? He's meditating on this issue when suddenly, without warning, lust surges through him. Bridget raw against the carpet, her flesh clenched to his. The lad could have come downstairs at any moment. He could have heard their meaty groans.

Bill steadies himself – but surely everyone can see his hand trembling as he picks up a fry that Max dropped. The pig-tailed kid wiping the tables, she knows where that hand's been.

'Viv,' he says thoughtfully, 'that's a palindrome. Her name reads the same forwards and backwards. Today's a palindrome. The tenth of November, 10/11/01. And how about this one? *It was a cat I saw.*' He starts writing down letters and numbers, training mind over matter, the matter of his cock, primed in his pants.

He can't believe his luck in finding Bridget. She had no need, surely, to answer his advert, a woman soft and warm and sexy, she'd have no problems attracting a man. So what does she see in Bill? Five foot six, his hair falling out, his job at Yellow Pages secure but unrewarding. He makes her feel protected, so she says. But there was nothing safe about last night.

'Thankyou for the meal,' says Max. He's like a little goblin, perched on the edge of his plastic seat. That hat annoys Bill. Next time, he's going to make him take it off.

Two o'clock. Another hour to fill. 'What would you like to do next, Max? How about the museum? Would you like to see the mummies?'

Max shrugs, stuffing the wrappers back into the box.

'I know what we can do. Where's the best ice cream in town?'

Max wonders if this could be a trick question. In town, ice cream's expensive. *There's plenty in the freezer. You can wait till we get home.*

Again. 'What's your favourite ice cream?'

Max goes for the unattainable. 'Baskin Robbins.'

'Where do you get that from?'

'Millie's. In the Arndale Centre.' Where he has often tried to linger on the way to buy new shoes.

Outside, it's started drizzling. The leaden street slides past them, like a dream. This is one of those wintery days when the sun never makes an appearance, and the sky seems lit by a thirty-watt bulb. Absent-mindedly, Max takes Bill's hand, then he lets go. Something stuck in his shoe is biting at his toe. He squashes his foot around, so it doesn't hurt so much. One lace is trailing in the puddles.

'Do you know,' says Bill, 'half a million people live in Manchester. Where do you suppose all these people are going? You know, Manchester hardly existed two hundred years ago. Max, have you ever tasted brown bread ice cream? Sounds funny, doesn't it? Actually it tastes delicious. We'll make some one day. When you come to my house. And vanilla – what's called vanilla ice cream very rarely is, these days. Vanilla's the pod of a plant that grows in Madagascar. If you ever have vanilla ice cream, check the label. and see if it's real. If it says 'vanilla flavouring', it isn't real vanilla ice cream. It's artificial, made out of chemicals.'

Rachel's got to come. She's bringing *Terminator*. It's really going to happen. Max gives a little skip as they pass through the glass doors into the warmth of the Arndale.

Max isn't so bad. He's a bright little chap, slightly introverted maybe. That's to be expected from an only child. Bridget shouldn't worry. Bill knows from his own experience, a certain kind of child thrives in solitude. He probably does a lot of reading. A bit of a dreamer.

What about the father? Bridget's saying nothing. No birthday card, no calls, no Sunday visits. If he makes her feel protected, why won't she tell the truth? She knows all his secrets, for what that's worth. And he's broadminded. She must know that by now.

'What's it going to be?' They've reached the flashing lights at Millie's stall. 'A double? What would you like?'

Max doesn't hesitate. 'Bilberries and cream. With almond and pistachio.'

A sophisticated choice, though, personally, Bill wouldn't match nut flavours with a fruit. He observes the surgical manner with which the Baskin Robbins girl slips a plastic bag over her hand.

'Pistachios,' he says, 'are very good in baked apples. It's funny, isn't it, how food that's the same colour always seems to go together. Now what shall I have? What do you think Jamoca is?'

'I need the toilet.'

'Yes yes, well hurry.' He watches the girl probing the big pastel tubs with her scoop. 'Be quick or your ice cream'll melt.'

When Bill was a child he was not allowed ice cream. Now he's grown up, he can eat what he likes, but only the best, not the dense Walls bricks he used to dream about, the penny scoops and forbidden raspberry ripples. It's Hagen-Daz now, or Loseley's with acacia honey; Marks and Spencer cappuccino, Thornton's double chocolate, or, if he's slumming, frozen Bounties – not forgetting the home made varieties he's promised to show Max. That's something they can do. They can make ice cream together.

The tiny piece of grit drops onto the floor from his sock, and is gone. This is Max's first time in the Men's. Usually, he goes with Bridget to the Ladies. He's finished, but he stays where he is for a while, flexing one bare foot in the air, and listening to the gruff sounds beyond the door.

Terminator comes back as a good guy. He promises not to kill people, just throw them around until they've learnt their lesson. That's not VIOLENCE. Who says that it's VIOLENT? Bridget never listens. Terminator belongs to this boy, and this boy can get him to do what he wants because, one day, this boy's going to save the world.

His machine brain whirrs into action as he goes through the routine of pulling up his pants, tying his laces, pretending to wash at the basin. His jaw stiffens. Back on the mall, he breathes deeply, feeling his muscles swell like balloons. He growls to himself in his Terminator voice. This way, guys.

Suddenly, Bill feels uneasy. She said something, whispering through the car window. Don't let him go to the toilet on his own. It isn't safe, she said. There's all kind of perverts. Bill's vision jumps like a damaged video. The subdued indoor noise of the Arndale runs dimly through his head. He starts running, greenish purple ice cream dripping down his sleeve.

This way. Maybe not. Trouble is, every shop Max walks by looks the same. Clothes, jewellery, shoes, bags and clothes, jewellery, shoes. But you always go past Millie's, whichever way you walk. Don't worry. *No problemo.*

Bill's not even sure what Max is wearing. The hat, that's all, the hat that hides his face. He's just looking for some kind of kid-sized hole in the crowd. A hole with a hat. He rushes through the toilets, pushing at the metal doors, calling out his name. All kinds of perverts. He could have been abducted. And who would be to blame? She'd never forgive him.

Bill made her feel protected. She put her trust in Bill. He asked her once, 'Shouldn't we be using something?' but she ignored him, rutting drunkenly in the darkness, not speaking, like he could have been anybody. He asked her again, and she said, 'I'm safe, aren't you?'

Bill's feet are slipping on the pale tiles. Somewhere a piano's playing *Strangers in the Night*.

'Here,' he says, 'have this,' ramming Max's cornet at a toddler in a pushchair. He starts shoving his way up the downwards escalator.

He has vanished by the time Max reaches Millie's. If he doesn't turn up, Max will have to find the Lost Children. There'll be an embarrassing announcement. There was one running now, in a teacherly voice. WILL THE MOTHER OF TYLER PARKER PLEASE COME TO THE INFORMATION DESK WHERE HER LITTLE GIRL IS WAITING. Max would rather die. He'd rather spend eight hours in Dolcis looking for new shoes. He circles Millie's stall again. If he tries hard enough, he's bound to conjure up the bald man in a coat. He has to do it. The alternative just isn't bearable.

Forget Terminator. He'd give up anything, just to be home. He keeps thinking about the way the cat always cries at the living room door. Unless you push it wide open, she doesn't believe she can come through. And the way she catches spiders, crunching them like twiglets.

An old lady's bending over him, asking if he's lost. 'No,' he says, 'not exactly,' trying to think of a way to explain.

Only a few minutes have passed, but it's like Bill's been searching for hours. He's cold with sweat. His head aches from the bitter, shadowless lighting. He's leaning against a metal banister, high above the place his search began, so afraid he can't even name his fears. The pianist has switched to *Smoke Gets in Your Eyes*, and he thinks he can hear the sound of running water. Then his own name is being called from below.

Max supposes he'll be shouted at. Which won't be fair, but will soon be over. Bill is definitely looking very angry, travelling slowly down the escalator to where Max is still standing with the old lady. His face, gone red, looks squashed and round. After thanking the old lady, he sweeps the cap from Max's head, and stares at him hard before speaking.

'So what do you think you've been up to?'

Something gets in the way of Max's voice, like the sharp piece of grit that was once in his shoe.

'Never mind. We'll forget about it. I won't tell your mother. Just don't ever wander off again.'

Bill's very quiet on the way home, in his big, silent car with the electronic windows. Max watches the intricate dials, still not sure how deeply he's in trouble. Things can't be that bad, if he's allowed to sit up front.

'Mum's one of those things,' he ventures.

'Sorry?'

'The same backwards and forwards. So's "dad".'

'You're right,' says Bill, 'a palindrome,' keeping his gaze steady, his hands just barely touching the controls.

Max sinks a little deeper into the seat. Eased by the car's

motion, his limbs are softening. He's almost asleep.

'I wonder what Mummy's done to her hair,' Bill ponders. 'She might surprise us.'

Max is starting to dream now. Behind his lids, he can see the darkness flowing.

'We won't say anything about that little mishap. I think you've learnt your lesson.'

Bilberries and cream. Pistachio. Maple fudge and almond. Max is sharing his ice cream with the Terminator. Terminator glugs with laughter. Not so bad, eh Max! But you better keep it a secret!

Bill glances at the sleeping child. How young Max is, much younger than Bill could ever imagine. He's looking into another man's eyes, through that face. Yet the pulse beating in the flesh is Bridget. He can even trace her in the way the boy's nose twitches in his dream, a nose whose shape is nothing like her own. To tell the truth, Max is an ugly little sod. A snub nosed hobgoblin. But he's not a bad little chap on the whole. They should do this again. Now they're getting used to one another. Make it a habit.

SEX ETC.

Things I can't do

Can't swim.
Can't drive.
Crap at spelling.

Although I can type. I'm typing this. And the machine fixes the miss takes. With a quick blink before you've even noticed. At first site I look like anyone else. I don't think I'm bad looking. I know that I'm knot. But theirs something different about me, something missing. You can tell.

If you think I've got one of those syndromes the dog who barked or something that's not what I'm saying. Nothing wrong with my brain. It's my hands and my fingers. I can't grasp things or keep hold of them. Objects some how slip aweigh. This caused problems when I was still at school. When I held out my tray for dinner the plate always missed. I have never caught a ball in my hole life.

You must be good at something

So they say. And I can cook. Surprisingly I can cook. Spaghetti. Proper Italian. Simmered for hours in a proper wine sauce. But Laura's a vegetarian. She can not meet eat.

I can't cook without making a mess. Tomato spattered all over my Strokes T-shirt witch cost me fifteen quid. I 'm hopeless.

Patrick you are hopeless.

I don't know how to get tomato from my clothes. Not knowing how is different from not being able to.

How to roll a joint.

Laura says: 'Watch'. She lays out rizlas, tobacco, the grass folded into a little square of cellophane like something you keep stamps in. Tears a piece off an old train ticket. 'Are you watching?' Fills the papers with tobacco, sprinkles on the grass, and now she licks it swiftly like a cat. 'Sea, it's easy. Now you do it.'

Try.

I can not concentrate.

That's how I ended up hear. I can't listen. Can't stick to one thing at a time. What are the reasons for Hamlet's delay… And instead of just giving the short answer I went off on one. When I looked up the teachers were already pacing round, glancing at the clock impatiently. Time was up. I was predicted to get a grade B for English, but I got a D. Could have stayed at home and retaken the exam. But I couldn't wait, could I? I wanted to grow up. So I decided to go into clearing.

Laura is an old black and white film, scene it once with Bernadette. That was how we spent our Saturdays, watching movies back to back, eating spaghetti and ice cream. Bernadette taught me all about Film Noir, Nouvelle Vague, Dogme – I can spell them all. I even picked up French from John Luke Goddard. No idea what letters make the sounds, but I can say the words in that shrug-your-shoulders accent. And I know what it means when a French bird turns to a bloke and says –

Forget it. Fill that one inn yourself.

Clearing

Strange word: Clearing. Like your in the jungle listening out for something stirring in the shadows, something or some one watching you waiting to spring.

What Clearing actually means off course is ticking off long lists of codes and figures and picking up the phone speaking to some one who pretends they aren't desperate to have you. Or you're mother does it for you. There are hundreds of universes, places you never heard of, and thousands of degrees in everything under the son. University of East and West. University of Smalltown, the Institute of Nowhere, the Universities of Narnia and Camelot, and the one I chose: Suffrage.

'Cross that one off,' said Bernadette, 'it's too far. You'd never get home for the weak end.'

Exactly.

Bernadette always liked a drink when she was watching the movies. When I got to round about thirteen or fourteen she'd pour a glass for me two. Then she'd have to fetch another bottle.

'What do you think of this one? Not too okay is it? Quite drinkable really. Three for a tenner'

Things I can't do

Walk on air
Raise the dead.
Turn water into wine
Or wine to water.
No one can.

Bernadette said, 'Its nice just the too of us. I'm lucky. You're better company than any blasted feller.' And then she'd squeeze me tight and say lets have another.

I do miss my mother. I feel sorry for her. But I wish she'd get a boy friend. I suppose she's just like me. There are things that some of us can't seem to manage, things that seem dead simple to everyone else. Sex etc.

Forrest Caught

They put me into Forest Caught overlooking knot a forest but fields. Fields, stretching further than the human eye can sea. The earth is flat round hear, like in those films where the helicopter sweeps over some guy running, running, maybe he's escaped from prison but there's no where to go. I'm not saying Suffrage University's like prison. Its all write, I like it hear, accept at night when you can't get to sleep, the running and yelling and footballs banging down the corridor, the flocks of girls screeching and the guys booming laughter rumbling past. And then the fire alarm just when you're dropping off.

I can sleep threw anything.

I used to be able to sleep threw anything.

One of those like Scott   Sleep threw anything. Sleep threw an earthquake

Let me tell you about Scott. He was like the brick laying genius. Since he was a little kid his dad took him on jobs. Not just brick laying, plastering and putting indoors. Anything to do with the building trade, they were up for it. So by the time he went to college to get his qualification he had nothing left to learn. His teachers saw write away he had the speed and proficiency to make the championships. So they put him down for the regional heats. He was a big hero in our village. Everyone wanted to buy him a pint. On the morning of the finals in Leeds, he overslept. His dad give him a knock: 'Yeah Dad, five minutes'. Then he hammered on the door hard: 'I know, I'm getting up, talk about waking the dead. Then his dad thought I can't be arsed. That'll learn him, little sod. So Scott is late. He's late, and it's the biggest moment in his life. He jumps into the car revs the engine – and wham. Head on collision. When the please turn up they say we're not touching him no chance. This one's had it. His skull was cracked like an egg. Like an egg with all the bits of shell sticking to the white. But this girl in a mini, she's stopped her car, and she's tearing off her blouse, her skirt, everything, and wrapping it round his head, trying to stop the blood and brains from spilling out. She saved his life. She wouldn't let them give up on him. Stayed with him all the way. Of course, Scott won't ever be the same. He can't lay bricks to start with, and there are other things to. Like remembering names and telling the time. He snoozes most of the day on the so far, and his dad stays at home in the chair.

Laura said: 'I couldn't do that could you?'

'What?'

'What that girl did. I can't stand the site of blood. I past out when I cut my finger once peeling potatoes.'

Some one else said: 'You don't know what you'd do if you had to. It's like that man who cut his arm off. His own arm. This mountain climber, his arm was trapped under these rocks and he knew he'd had it if he couldn't free himself.'
'Is that true? You didn't see it on the telly?'

I often think about the girl at the roadside stripped to her bra and panties splashed in blood. Hair falling round her face. Laura's face.

We were standing outside Forest Caught waiting for the all clear. No chance of a reel fire, never was. which must have been a piss off for the local fire brigade. Standing there, that was how I first got talking to Laura.

'Hey,' she said, 'your going to trip on your laces.'

I pretended they were like that on purpose.

'Did you know that lad? The one in the accident?'

'Kind of. My mum was going out with his dad – it was a few years ago like.'

'How awful.'

'Yeah.'

Etc. etc.

Thought I stayed pretty cool.

Laura

So? Laura. As the sun rose over the flat endless fields, I went back into my room and tapped out the five letters of her name. And then I just sat there starring at the screen. And tapped the space bar once, twice, easing the cursor further along passed all the empty spaces like a brick wall standing there where I tried to describe her
but couldn't
so you'll just have to imagine her, like I did before I even met her.

Questions (1)

Where are you from?

What are you studying?

Are you going to the Pit on Wednesday?

'Why would I do that?'

'It's where everyone goes.'

'So why would I want to?'

I can't get anywhere with Laura. She answers questions with more questions. Circling round the answers like a boxer.

'How come,' she says, 'I never saw you before? You're in the same class as me and the same hole of residence?'

I tell her I' m the invisible man.

'One minute,'

she says and with a strange satisfied smile she holds her phone up to her face like a mirror, tapping a massage back to whoever it is who is tasting her.

Questions (2)

Is Hedda Gobbler a sympathetic character?

How does Ibsen subvert audience expectations?

I have actually read the book so I have an advantage over most of the class and over Laura who has red most of it but doesn't have a copy.

'I don't get it, she says. 'What does it mean subvert? What do they want us to say?'

She frowns at the computer screen. 'Your spelling's shit.' And then she laughs. 'What is this, Hedda Gobbler? O I know. You got this from the film, write?'

'What do you mean?'

'Hedda GOBBLER? Cum on your shitting me. I herd it before. It's from a film.'

I'm leaning over her shoulder as she points at the name I've spelled wrong. Close enough to smell her skin, nearly touching, easier than breathing, grazing on her hair and nibbling her ear, easy, she wouldn't even notice. and the little cursor winks at me, I can hardly stand it, then she turns around.

'God which film is it? Hang on.'

She texts some won then shakes her head.

'Is it bollocks. No it isn't Sideways. Something else, what is it? This is really pissing me off. Don't you hate it when you have this weird shape in your head and you know what it is but it just keeps drifting round the edges. Hedda Gobbler.'

It isn't all that funny.

But at least I can spell Header Gabler now.

Questions (3)

Fine.

Its cool.

Okay.

Not especially no.

I am. Yes. Really. Course I will

How's work? What you been up to?

What has she been up to? Bernadette never goes anywhere since she lost her driving license. She had her chances. What happened to Scott should have been a warning. And then there was the time she was sent on a training course for drivers who can't resist speed. But her foot presses down on the peddle and zoom, she's looping round the bend. She thinks she's special. What applies to others does not apply to her. 'It isn't the miles per hour that kills, just all the rotten drivers.'

She feels so bad that she couldn't bring me here like all the other parents. She wants to no exactly what it's like. She wants to play the pictures in her head. Patrick the student. She wants to stop the clock at any point in the day. Close her eyes and bee hear by my side.

Because how I'm going to take care of myself she cannot for the life of her imagine.

'Patrick, Patrick, you're underpants are showing.'

And every time I swear every fucking time I tell her that's how their meant to look and does she listen?

'Don't be daft I know what your like. You just can't fasten your belt properly, can you?' She grabs hold of my trousers and hoists them back up. 'No wonder. Their too sizes two big.'

Then she reaches both arms around my waste and squeezes. 'My boy. My handsome big boy.' And lays her head against my chest and we stay there like some statue on a war memorial.

Sex Etc
Obviously I am not a virgin. I am not a total twatt. I have done it. Once or twice.

But lets not get into that.

Cock and Bull
'Cock and Bull!   That's where it comes from. Cock and Bull Story!'

At first I don't get what she's on about. Then I remember. So that's all she wants the only reason she could possibly cum knocking in the middle of the knight.

'This character Steve Cooogan plays, well its himself really, he gets caught with this prostitute and she's called Header Gobbler. Sorry Patrick. Were you in bed?'

She looks all round my room, casts her eye on the clothes piled on the floor and my Stroke CDs tumbling across the desk and my John Luke Goddard poster all within seconds because that's all it takes.

'I just wanted to tell you that's all,'

'Did you have a good weak end?'

'Yeah cool. Weight till you see what my dad got me. I'll let you have some if you skin up. Can you do it yet? Did you practice like I told you?'

I've noticed this about Laura, how she's always wide a wake. Even at 9 o'clock lectures when her eyes seem to slither in her head from staying up late she's still awake looking startled and surprised.

'How about you? Hey Patrick, scene my wring?' She wriggles her fingers at me. 'I'm engaged.'

Things to do on Saturday
Look for a job. Something which does not involve stacking objects or collecting empty glasses.
Shopping. But I don't need anything.
Watching a movie.
Finishing my essay on HEDDA GABLER
Not going home.
Waiting for Sunday when Laura comes back.
Not going home.
Sod it, lets go home.

Home
Bernadette works for social services. She thinks of herself as a

practical person. But she isn't not really. She will have a go but she doesn't know what she's doing. There's still no bathroom door because Scott's dad never came back to finish the job. 'I'm going to get round to hanging that door,' she says every Easter and Christmas and August Bank Holiday. 'It won't take long once I put my mind two it.'

'I got your favourite,' she says, 'fig roles,' and then she can't find where she put them and she empties out everything in the cupboard. Not a lot there accept wine bottles and wry vita and old tins of beings because Bernadette is trying to loose wait. But still she can't find that packet of biscuits. 'Maybe I just went in the shop and forgot what I came for. But I wouldn't of done, not if I went in specially. Or maybe I left them behind when I was packing.'

She can not stop talking. I'm sorry. She can't. She can not shut up even when we're supposed to be watching a Korean film concerning too monks on a lake. And looking at me. Can't stop that either. 'O Patrick' she says, 'we do have some good times. Lets crack open another bottle.'

And then there is a huge crash because she was standing on the work surface groping on top of the cub board looking for the fig roles.

Back too Normal

Bernadette is not badly hurt. But she is suffering from Massive Bruising. So now it's my turn to be in charge. She sleeps most of the day and comes down in the evening to watch the telly or a DVD. We agree Cock and Ball's not bad for a British film.

Quite clever.

'You are going back?' says Bernadette. 'What about your teachers?'

They won't notice. I told you, I can be invisible. But I wonder about Laura.

And yes, I think I will go back next weak when Bernadette gets better. I'll get back very late, and there she'll be, Laura, she'll be their and she'll say 'Where were you?' in that cross accusing voice.

I'll say 'Did you miss me?'

'Didn't you get my message?'

'I can't text.'

'What?' She'll bend down and tie my laces. 'What do you mean, you can't text? Patrick, what are you like?'

STORY SWAP

If I am anyone, then I'm conducting a seminar on Borges, at seven o'clock on the eleventh of August 1999, in Waterstone's on Deansgate.

You'll find me in a small room at the very top of the building, round the corner from Kafka's coffee bar, between the business, crime and children's sections. There's a customer toilet tucked away here, if you want to search for it, avoiding the gaze of your fellow punters; unlike in Woody Allen films, eyes rarely meet across the stacks. Bookshops are furtive places, voyeuristic. You're opening books you can't afford – browsing, not reading, handling each at a distance, like pornography. Next door, in a larger room, a distinguished writer's making an appearance. As the ticketholders enter, the big room bates its breath.

In the small room, the punters are learned and excitable. We're discussing how rarely Borges refers to sensual experience, how he seems to dwell entirely in the catacombs of the mind. And how interesting it is that such a mandarin should have influenced, more than anything, films and popular culture and that, if he has influenced literature it's through those baggy volumes by Marquez and Eco, and not his own genre, short fiction. There are bottles of red wine, white wine, mineral water and juice on the table. I'm on the red.

As I lead the conversation, I can see myself reflected in the dark glass partition between the meeting room and the corridor. I'm mesmerised by my own gestures. Most teachers are clowns and contortionists, underlining the big words in bold. I watch the roll of my wrists as I grasp some huge and invisible box, hold it in front of them, there, ladies and gentlemen, before your very eyes...

My German teacher used to bang into the classroom, announcing himself fiercely. 'Smith is here!' Herr Schmidt dressed formally, in a suit, *sehr ungewöhnlich* for a young man this late in the century – like a tall, dark question mark. I spent my dinner hours swotting in the Arboretum, lying among the daisies, reading the *Urfaust*. Once he spotted me there. He suddenly reared above me, as choppy and fierce as ever. 'I see,' he sneered, 'so this is what you're up to. Picking up men in the park.' I was baffled. I thought Herr S liked me. I wouldn't have been in the sixth form if he hadn't talked my parents into letting me stay on.

I wouldn't be here now, inventing ridiculous theories. There are very few women in Borges. You could say that we're the ultimate secret society. Why are women so apparently like other human beings, and yet possessed by such mystical powers? In 'The Circular Ruins' a magician thinks a boy into existence, but in doing so must destroy himself. Not so women. We are infinite. In fact, the whole of Borges's oeuvre may be regarded as a response to the feminine – an attempt to super-impose an admittedly inadequate masculine ordering onto the chaos of lived experience.

Bollocks I know, but I thought I'd test it out. Some one must protest - the gnome who's read every book in existence or the librarian with the hushed voice – but no, the group listens respectfully, then some one throws in a better idea, and the argument runs on ahead.

I write. This is why I earn my living in this way, running

the odd session, banging on about things I don't know much about. I swap stories, sometimes, with a friend. If she wrote them herself, she'd be ostracised in her village, because they're all true. There's the story, for instance, of the doctor's wife who had Parkinson's. She kept pills in her purse, ready to die when the time came. In fact she stayed well, just the odd tremor, now and then. The dark angel passed by. Until the doctor fell in love with some one else.

But the story I'm working on isn't this one. It's a science fiction story. In the world that I have conjured, no one's middle aged. There are only the ancient immortals, a few children and teenagers, who are extremely susceptible to disease. The youngsters festoon themselves with parasites, a kind of tic that fastens onto the arms and neck, changing colour as it fills with blood, like a ripening grape. Very bad for your health – but the youngsters won't listen. And one thing's for sure, they won't stop having babies. That won't ever stop. But what about the story, how does it end? I don't know.

The doctor's story is much simpler. His wife couldn't open the purse. Her fingers went numb, and she couldn't work the catch. But she did somehow manage to pull a carrier bag on her head. The man did not remarry. His mother was ninety-seven years old, speechless, incontinent and blind. He took her from the home and nursed her, giving up his practice to keep her from the grave. When she had another stroke, the hospital suggested withholding treatment. He refused.

Outside, it's still light. There's a bout of drilling so loud we have to stop the discussion, and it's during this pause that I scribble down something that might end up in this story. Since the bombing, Manchester's been incessantly rebuilding. The skyline's dominated by spindly cranes, like storks, delivering exclusive malls and grand hotels at every junction. Large hoardings depict the Promised Land. In the coming century, there will be palm trees and fountains and eternal light. Empty warehouses are being scrubbed and gutted, kitted out for the incomers who toil in the creative industries. Some streets have vanished. Others have been repositioned in the middle of the map, rather than its margins, as the city centre pushes further out towards the backwoods. I have a poor sense of direction at the best of times. I find myself accidentally taking the long way round, circling another shrouded crater, where plate glass and granite are destined to rise. Sometimes I feel as if I just stepped off a plane. I'm a tourist in my own city.

The celebrity reading is still going on. As we leave the smaller room, we can hear the writer's voice remotely, and appreciative murmurs ripple through the white gloss door. The group's very loyal to stick with me tonight. The shop itself is empty, all except for the books of course, all those books, thousands, crowding the dark shelves; walls of books, piles of them crammed on tables, ranged in display racks, and none of them by me.

Because I can't finish, can I? I can't ever reach the end. Years ago I started a novel. In those days I lived in a basement. Every morning, I hunched over my electric typewriter, breaking off every hour or so to walk up the thirteen steps to the kitchen, make myself a brew, and bring it back downstairs. From Spring to Autumn, I wrote and rewrote, each sentence etched by diamonds, and then I'd start that perfect opening all over again. Now the words themselves seem to perish. The stories get shorter, the sentences more clipped. There's something more to add that always escapes me.

My school, the girls' school, was cobbled together out of what used to be the boys' school, both its Victorian section and the science block added in the nineteen-thirties; and a modern single-storey annexe at the back. The whole complex was surrounded by seven foot walls. In the fifth form, you were granted the privilege of entering through the main gate, instead of round the side. Once you reached the sixth form, you were even allowed to walk through the front door. We were considered mature enough to pass by the headmistress's office without causing offence. We were even let off the grounds at lunchtime, so long as we upheld the school's reputation. Eating, for instance *war strengst verboten.*

There were very few male teachers, and still fewer young ones like Herr Schmidt. The school was run by spinsters, who reminded us at all times that we were the lucky ones. We had been chosen, given opportunities, for which we should offer thanks by being of service to society at large. I always believed I was there by mistake. There'd been some kind of mix-up in the eleven plus, and one day I'd be found out. That's why I swotted in the park, instead of doing things other teenage girls were up to, such as smoking and having sex.

But you know all this, don't you? I don't have to go on. It's been written in numerous notebooks. It's scribbled on envelopes, bus tickets and beer mats; typed in Courier, Tahoma, Garamond and Times New Roman; copied onto unreadable disks, and stored in obsolete Amstrads.

The Borges story I think about most, and whose title, of course, I can never remember, is the one about the man whom God grants another year to complete his masterpiece, within the very second that he's put to death. Borges is perfect for me. Because I can't finish reading a book any more than I can write one. Books are piled by my bedside, postcards and tickets stuck in their pages, marking the place where I left off – *The Count of Monte Cristo* and *Gulliver's Travels*, *Daniel Deronda* and *The Pillow Book* – hardbacks and soft covers, and fusty pocket editions. *Everyman I will go with thee to be thy guide, in thy most need to go by thy side.*

To make a story, something has to change. You have to find yourself somewhere else when you turn the last page. This is the story I gave to my friend. My uncle had been married for nearly forty years – going to work, coming home, shopping with the family on Saturday. One week, in W.H. Smith's, he spotted a guidebook to Florida. They'd been to Florida before, but who knows? There might be something new in it, something they had yet to discover.

As soon as they got home the argument started. What do you want to do that for? Throwing away money on a book! My uncle sat listening to my aunt, then he turned to her and said, 'You hate me don't you? I know we don't love each other. That's long gone. But you really can't abide me. We ought to get divorced.'

At this time of year, the streets are not so busy, open and free without the students, who'll come back in autumn like migrating birds, settling the length of Oxford Rd and on as far as Cinecity. Nobody likes the ones who come up from the south, complaining in strident voices about their alleged poverty, swarming through the cut price drinking dens laid on especially for them. What if something happened? Supposing people turned on the students, suppose they were hunted, like aristocrats in the French Revolution? Where would they go? Who would hide them?

What a bonfire they'd make, all those ideas that don't go anywhere, those notes shoved into drawers, all those lost plots and flimsy descriptions. One day, I'll scrap the lot and start again, and next time I might even tell the truth. I wasn't being completely honest about Mr. Smith and the arboretum. I mean, in the picture I gave of myself. Of course I was smoking, of course I had sex, plenty of it. And yet I believed that I wouldn't get pregnant, that I was exempt, in the same way I believed I would never grow old.

When I catch the bus, some one from the group is sitting on the back seat reading – the librarian with the hushed voice and the silvery owl's hair. She must have got on at another stop, Piccadilly, I suppose. She says how much she's enjoying the sessions, and are there any books I'd recommend on Borges?

She's got me now, because I don't actually know very much about Borges. I just made it up. So I muse, and then I tell her there might be one or two. 'Or why don't you could just read *Don Quixote* and Kafka, Sherlock Holmes and Robert Louis Stevenson and the Koran and Kipling. Read what he read.'

'I'd never catch up with him.'

'Never.'

What I especially like about that particular Borges story – the one about the lost masterpiece – is that the merits of the great work are never under discussion. The poor guy put everything, his life and soul, into this project – which is the same for everyone, whether you're a genius or an absolute no-hoper, so who can tell the difference in the end?

I first read Borges in hospital, when I was still young, and expected to do quite a lot with my life. I borrowed *Labyrinths* from my boyfriend at the time, some one I learnt a lot from, when we were living in the basement. I learnt to love Borges. But I didn't love the boyfriend, not enough to have his baby. Children should be born from love. And that's why I'm childless. But I always remember, in August, the child that might have been, one year older – eighteen, nineteen, twenty-one – as the century turns.

It's dark and quiet at the end of the line. I'm the last one on the bus. I get off where the road suddenly comes to a full stop at the edge of the meadows, where the plans for a motorway link have been cancelled. I can't wait to be home, close the door, turn on the lights and start again, rejecting the other stories for the sake of this one, which is going to tell you everything you thought you had forgotten.

TWENTIETH FRAME

1. Light knifes through the open window. My head aches from the train journey, and now from George's talk, driving too fast round the lanes. '…In a few years it'll pay for itself…' Her arm stretched towards the farthest corner of the glass, she leans out, Windolene in hand. Scarf on head. Without hair, a face as innocent as a baby doll. I screw my eyes to catch the round eyes and the mouth in the sun. When she sees us coming she waves. She smiles, but she keeps herself vacant. You must be Joyce.

2. George. Not yet thirty-five, you would think him born forty. A man who digs slowly at his, the largest, serving of mash and roast meat; carefully he measures each well-proportioned chew. Master of the meal, he is the last to finish. By his slowness and stealth he seems a natural countryman. Joyce and I, compelled to wait, smile hesitantly at each other and finger the stems of our wine glasses. We sit opposite each other at the pine table. George sits at the head.

    'Did you have a good journey?' she asks at last, her voice a trickle in the pinot blanc I brought with me.

    'Not too bad,' I reply – netted in the clichés of small talk. I state the connections and delays that brought me to the Dorset countryside, not forgetting the side issues of the weather on the crossing.

    'You didn't fly then?'

    'I like the ferry.'

'So you won't be using the Channel Tunnel?'

'If it's ever built.'

'It will be,' George grunts.

'What's it like, living in France?' she asks brightly. I don't tell her about the smell of decay in the classroom, the schoolboy sniggers in the silence between bells; I don't tell her how when I'm alone in my flat I feel the walls are watching me. No, I tell her about the charms of a French town, the wine and the market days – which, gazing at the almost empty bottle, I genuinely miss. It's strange how your environment refuses to be marked by your own unhappiness. I have lost the rhythms of my own speech. My English is strained. Formal. She soon stops listening, although she wants to be interested by me.

'Finished?' she says to George. George has lain down his knife and fork side by side on the empty plate. She herself has eaten less than half her dinner. The remainder she tips into a bowl for the dog who leaps from her chairside to eat it. I noticed when I arrived how she took a digestive with her tea, only to nibble at the edge and throw the rest to him.

The pudding is rhubarb crumble, coated with thick yellow custard. School dinner, but well cooked. I doubt that, left to herself, Joyce would eat like this. Small and light as a lettuce leaf, she scarcely seems capable of managing a farm all by herself.

We don't talk till afterwards when George, sitting back in his chair, says: 'So what's the plan? Are you going straight on to Mom's after the weekend? Or coming to London with me? There's plenty to do on the farm if you fancy staying over. Give Joyce a hand. Do you good to use your muscles for a change.'

3. 'She seems a nice enough girl,' our mother wrote. 'I hope
George hasn't made any promises to her.'

Joyce said: 'You aren't how I expected. You aren't like
your brother.'

'I'm the quiet one.'

'George is quiet.'

'Thoughtful,' I said.

'Yes. George isn't very forthcoming – but we're very
happy together.' She said it as if I didn't know George – as if
I were her brother, and she had to explain him to me. 'I'm
putting a lot into this relationship, and a lot into the farm. We
both are.'

'I can see that.'

'She used to be an infant teacher,' wrote our mother. 'So
how she's going to manage on a farm I don't know. There's
some things you can't learn out of books.'

4. I was leaning against the bookshelves filled with her books.
Some were the English classics – Lawrence, George Eliot –
Hardy of course. Then there were those feminist books
women read at launderettes when I was a student – *The
Female Eunuch, The Feminine Mystique, The Second Sex*. A
few detective stories. And some large hardbacks, carefully
bound with cellophane, on livestock breeding and veterinary
science. They were all hers. George never read.

He sat in his armchair, staring hard at Joyce. She had
come from her bath in a flowered robe. She sat curled up,
twisting strands of her damp brown curls and pulling at her

pink toes, reading an orange Penguin. I couldn't quite see the title.

George couldn't stand watching people read. He dropped his *Exchange and Mart* on the floor and picked it up again, still keeping his eyes on her. The dog, stretched out with his nose between his front paws, watched him sadly in return. I carried on reading the titles of books, idly searching for clues to Joyce's life. It whiled away the time.

George stood up suddenly. 'Let's go to the Dragon.'

The houseplants, the pastel prints and the craft shop pottery – they would be Joyce's too. I'd expected a damp, stonebuilt cottage, bought cheap for the dream of land. In fact the house was as spacious as any Reagan ranch house, as airy as a colonial bungalow. The big grate and the wall cupboards had been built into a house too comfortable to be more than a few years old. George must have had more money than I thought.

'I'm worried about George,' Mom used to say. 'He's so easily taken advantage of.' To George, she used to say: 'I'm worried about Geoffrey. He's so secretive.' I knew what she'd say. She'd talk as she wiped over the mantelpiece or folded the washing, moving within the endless rhythms of domestic drudgery. George would not be listening. 'Has he said anything to you about a girlfriend?'

George in his sheepskin jacket swung the car keys round his fingers. 'You don't want to come, do you Joyce?'

Joyce wasn't listening.

5. No sleeping in strange houses. My own terror binds me to this narrow plank of a bed, tilting in the unlived space of the

spare room.

Froth on George's red mouth. 'What about you Geoff, eh? Any more luck?' A regular row of teeth, but the eyes on the small side. Is he good-looking? Better than me? Impossible to tell what women like in a man. Impossible to deny that he's healthy enough, healthier than me.

In the face of ugliness, I think of Hannah. And as she rises to the surface, he says, 'Just keep away from the married women,' as if he knew all about that, and perhaps he does, but how I do not know, and will not ask, because he isn't interested anyway.

No good wanking either. I can't be soothed tonight. Instead I'm left edgy, sore and open to the night sounds. Even here, miles from the main road, I can hear cars in the darkness. I'd expected animals. Cattle lowing, hoots of owls, bat wings – but there is silence in between the passing engines. I'm alone here, balanced in this emptiness. There are no borders, no finishing point, no water left to cross.

And I'm dreaming now. I know I'm dreaming in my wakened sleep. I don't like the beer. I don't want it. It's salt, slopping against the metal sides. I dream of paralysis. I dream of closed doors and cold lavatories and voices behind the outhouse door, old women's voices and boys'. I understand French, I tell them. I know they're speaking French. But the sound is distorted and backward, a if my ears have become a strange mirror to the airwaves. I hear my voice saying, 'Just a half for me this time.'

Out of my dream. The darkness isn't entirely black when I look more closely. It's a cakey grey, crumbly like soil.

'...the French women,' says George. What is it he's saying?

'Why don't you come with me on Monday? Leave the old girl for a couple of days. You can have a night out in London. I can show you some places – there's things they'll do for you that haven't got names yet.'

I don't answer because I don't understand what he's talking about. Yet.

'Did I tell you I'm staying in a hotel now? Company's paying.' He sips his beer, thoughtful – as I said to Joyce, thoughtful – and he names the figure he's earning.

'What is it you do that's worth that amount of money?'

From behind his glass George smiles at me as if to say, come on Geoff, you should know. Or: the things I do for the money, you can't put a name to them yet. How unsporting of me to earn such a small figure myself.

'It's easy to make money,' says George, 'if you give them what they want.'

I believe him.

'Why can't you do well for yourself?' our mother says. 'You were always top at school, Geoffrey.'

'So when are you giving it up?' I ask.

He shrugs. 'Three years?'

'I thought you were earning this money to stop work, so you could be on the farm.'

'My money's still keeping this place. You don't know how much it costs to set yourself up.'

'So Joyce is going to have to carry on by herself.'

'She can manage. She's castrating the young calves tomorrow. There's nothing she can't do. I sent her to college, you know. She does well out of it, and I give her a wage.'

'She must get tired of it sometimes, and lonely on her own.'

'I'm here every weekend, Friday through to Monday. I work hard too you know. Besides,' he grinned, 'she's nuts about me. There's nothing she wouldn't do.'

I don't believe he can't afford to give up the capital and its unnamed attractions. I believe that if you really want something you can have it. That's why, I suppose, I can't really have wanted Hannah, to let her go without loving me.

6. Minutes? Hours? How long since I washed my face with pink soap and dried it with the towel left out for me? How long since I, naked, put my meagre body to bed? I heard something. An animal's cry. It drew itself out into a long moan, and then, raised higher in the air, at last became human. It subdued itself and stretched up again, anger was it or fear – the bitterness of pleasure? I waited to meet its rise again. I wanted to put the light on, but knew I mustn't.

I stuff my loose prick between my thighs, I tug at my pubic hair. I want to get away from the sound, but there is no hiding from it. The silence itself is an echo of the cry. I know it's only Joyce. I know it's a commonplace sound at night time, as usual as the flush of a toilet or the creak of bedsprings. Perhaps it's because there are none of those sounds that I'm afraid of this one. How could it be Joyce? I remember the practicality of the arm at the window. No sensuality in the crook of her elbow or the short-nailed, small-proportioned hands that served potatoes. 'The French women,' says George, 'are the French women what they're cracked up to be?' In London they can't even find names for it.

7. Without warning it becomes daylight. I don't remember falling asleep. Perhaps, after all, I slept well. I don't feel tired. I feel warm. I think it was the dog that woke me, running into my room and out again. The door has been pushed open, and from downstairs I can hear the clatter of busy people.

'Quiet, you'll wake your brother up.'

'It's about time he was woken up.'

As I turn the covers back, a rush of cold air meets between open door and window. Outside the bed, it's chillier than yesterday, damp. I put my glasses on to read my watch – is that all the time is?

'He's on holiday,' she says.

'His whole bloody life's a holiday,' he replies, pulling his boots on, tightening his belt, taking his tools in hand.

8. You will expect me to tell you how beautiful it was, and now it's time I did so. My brother's farm was deep inside a valley, cradled by soft Dorset hills that shadowed the clouds. The clouds themselves were so close that morning that we were caught inside them. I was reminded of other landscapes, just as a book will make me want another book, one meal will bring to mind another. I thought of the sea during the crossing – the solid grey armoury of waves on a dull day; and of great wedges of summer sunset against cathedral stone. Looking at the dark drawn green around me, I reflected that

it is the movement of light that is beautiful, but because of that fact I could never grasp beauty. Only the static is near to me. Only postcards can be sent through the mail.

The ten-week-old calves were dappled like the hills, in black and white and the ochre of their excrement. Like soppy pups, they gathered round Joyce, while the real dog raced round the pen, as if to show them what it was like to be a free individual. Sensing their lives through large tongues and nostrils, they waited faithfully for food, for water and for the eventual safety of the marketplace.

'You don't mind, do you?' said George. 'Might as well get it done while there's three of us.' (He must have been planning this when he asked me here.)

'You've done this before, haven't you?' I asked her.

'I came top in my exam,' she said. 'And I've done those' – nodding towards the bigger calves in the field. 'It's quite quick. There's no blood. It's for their own benefit really. They'd just get restless and hurt each other if they were left.'

Sunlight was seeping through the morning mist. It was getting warmer.

'Got your wellies?'

'I've brought walking boots.'

'You can borrow a pair of George's. And what about trousers?'

9. The photos. Here in the room at the centre of my brother. Joyce's tampons are at the side of the big duvet'd bed. On the other side, his large and newish tweed check slippers. Marks and Spencer's. For a long moment, I stand here looking for

clues. It's as near as I'll ever get to him.

Unless I am his executor. Strange thought, what makes me think of him suddenly, laid out with a smile on his lips? As if he were dead, I flatten this room into two dimensions. I slide open the fitted wardrobe gently, knowing snooping is wrong. I touch the clothes in the closet like turning the pages of a book. Then I open the drawer which George has told me holds the trousers.

The drawer beneath is open slightly. I know there is something inside for me. Blindfold, I would have seen it shimmer faintly.

Those seconds in which I open the drawer and take hold of my destiny are running on inside the time I continue to live. In my dreams, I will always pull the drawer slightly and stop, listening for a noise behind me. Quickly, as if speed made less of the deed, I snatch them out, scan them and drop them back inside, exactly where I found them. I leave the room with George's old trousers in my hand.

10. Photos. Do you want to know what they were?

The trousers were of brown corduroy. They were Marks and Spencer's too. Naturally, being George's, they were too loose and slightly too short, but luckily there was a broad belt on them.

A belt of the kind one imagines fathers taking to their sons. For looking at, or rather, being caught looking at, photos of this kind. My own father never took a belt to me. The punishment of children wasn't his job, and besides I never did anything serious enough to be handed over to a father. My mother's technique, when I broke an ornament or lost my pumps, or went near a canal, or put my hands in my pockets, was simply not to talk to me. Sometimes she would say: 'I never thought you would do this to me, Geoffrey.' She must have meant something else. Or somebody else. Now it's: 'I don't know why you won't settle down, Geoffrey.'

They were 1970s trousers, not in bad nick, but old-fashioned, flared. It felt wrong to wear them, as if I were making some hopeless attempt to impersonate the owner. I could see the sharp, angled reflection of my body when I put them on. In the mirror. The mirror above the drawer which held the photographs.

11. I strode along the wet grass, over the fence, towards the two of them. They were watching the calves, absorbed in money talk – the price of hay and the value of the fat, still living meat. Joyce turned to look at me as I drew nearer. She had those eyes that are not afraid to stare because they show nothing. I looked down at George's boots, loose on my feet.

'You ready then?' said George. He didn't say, 'You've been a long time.' He didn't ask me what I'd been up to. I don't think he remembered that I was on his property when he wasn't made to see me there.

All day long, it seemed, George and I held down the young calves. It was easy to stop being nervous of the animals if I thought of them, not as living creatures, but as lumps to be held, and they were still, except for the one who trod, absent-mindedly, on my foot. I felt their blood and their breathing like an engine running down.

'It's not bothering you?' said George.

I said no. It was his wrists that tightened every time

Joyce made the cut. He watched carefully as she, in silence and without bloodshed, eased the testes out of the flesh. The dog yapped and gulped at the fresh meat. She worked as deftly, as hypnotically, as a needlewoman.

At last the sun swung through the mist, turning the sky most definitely hot. Joyce tossed her curls from her eyes – no headscarf today. She didn't sweat. No moisture in the armpits of the shrunken pink T-shirt. There was a pile of manure, high as the house, next to the barn. As the calves waited their turn, liquid shit spurted out of their arses, and we splashed and rubbed against the dung as we worked. The whole place smelt sweet and rich with shit – like curry. At dinner time we stopped for chicken sandwiches. Joyce went back to the house to set the timer for our evening meal.

I was lost in the simplicity of the routine, the quick action of the knife and the dog's rapid disposal. I felt happy not to talk or think. I was contented to be here. Yet Joyce was the woman in the photographs.

12. I wanted to get away.

Joyce's round and shallow eyes magnify my own emptiness. I am cold inside.

She passes potatoes. My hands slip.

'Sorry. Is the dish hot?'

It is the meeting of our skins that I'm avoiding.

I am going to go back into that room.

Of course, you already know what's in the photographs.

There are genetic and social forces. Both are, to some extent, predictable. For instance, George and I both have the same, hardly perceptible, stoop – caused partly by the way our father walked, and partly by living for years in a small terraced house. Within this pattern, there's a flaw – there always is. But who's the flaw this time, myself or my brother?

On the one hand, Geoffrey. Geoffrey is an educated man. He takes a considered stand on subjects such as, let us say, pornography. He is in touch with the issues of the day – privatisation, the miners, the nuclear threat – having read the English papers once a week, a week behind. He holds strong views, though nothing extreme. But George on the other hand – what does George, the nearest neighbour of his flesh, make of it all?

Sex seems to be a good thing. Watching sex – perhaps not. Taking pictures of sex may be bad. Looking at such pictures certainly wrong. Well produced, I noticed. By George, presumably, since he isn't in any of them. Colour nicely balanced. I have something of an interest in photography, lacking as I am in artistic talent. I have taken photographs of, let's say, women's faces close to me. And their bodies. With the clothes discreetly on them.

When I saw Hannah naked, my eyes were not sufficient to my senses. When I smelt her skin, my breath was not big enough to take her in. She took me, and I was lost beyond the borders of photographic prints. That is why I kept no photographs of Hannah.

13. I am going back into the room.

'Oh well, time to feed the calves,' says Joyce, rousing herself from the corner.

And George: 'I'll come down with you. You know that

little one? There's something wrong with his eye.'

The room is exactly the same as I left it. No sign of disorder, the shoes lined up exactly, the bed uncrumpled. Everything in its place. Nothing by accident. How could the photographs be by accident?

George meant me to find them. There's a purpose in my coming here, and in the work we did today. Whatever the reason for their existence, whatever the business or pleasure, today he is using the photographs to show me how much he has at his disposal, while I have nothing, nothing to build or destroy. I peel a broken fingernail and place it under the bedclothes.

14. I have to leave. He knows about Hannah. I know how he found out, but that doesn't matter. It happened before I went abroad, the time before last that I visited our mother. I remember walking past the gasometer, the junior school and the clinic in the mid-afternoon. I got off a stop too early by mistake.

It wasn't that I was upset. Being upset had already happened. By now I'd grown bored with my own unhappiness, the brief melodramatics were over, and all that would happen to me was the same feelings stretching uselessly on. I was more tired out than anything. As I walked towards the house where I grew up, I thought I heard the sea. It seemed natural enough until I remembered exactly where I was – ninety miles from the nearest ocean. And landlocked for good.

'What's the matter?' she said across the tablecloth. 'You don't seem yourself Geoffrey.'

116

I started to cry, more from weariness than sorrow.

'It's some woman, isn't it?' she said.

I told her the truth, or at least half of it. It was easier than keeping silent. She sighed and said: 'You did the right thing in the end.' The facts I had told her were a disguise; and what I had done and decided was an illusion hiding all that might have been.

'You'll feel better now it's off your chest' – buttering bread for our tea.

Some woman. I've been in this bath so long, the water's cold and thick as snot, but I'm comfortable, moulding the lemon-scented soap round myself, thinking of the little grey hairs round Hannah's ears and her cast-off coats from Oxfam, always one size too big.

All around me, bottles of lavender, verbena, rosemary, the flowers of Joyce's unnatural innocence. Strange that she bothers with scents in a place overhung with the smells of manure, grass and engine oil – as strange as the Laura Ashley dresses that she harbours for some unlikely social occasion. Strange that she should be here at all, strange as nightmares of the grown up world to a child...

You've seen me naked. You know me. No need to describe me standing there, my body caked with cleanliness, sniffing at Joyce's lotions. No need to describe its shape or state at this moment on a summer Saturday. Dizzy, I reach for my glasses on the cistern. I dress slowly, ready to meet the two of them again. I walk downstairs.

Darkness is coming already. Although the curtains are still open, the lamp is lit. It is Joyce I see first, the long-spouted watering can in her hand. She's trying to water one of the numerous houseplants while behind her George is biting at her ear. He has his hands round her small body, she's ticklish, they're playing together. I can see her face reflected in the glass. They aren't embarrassed by their childishness. They don't stop because of me. I'm scarcely there at all, but for a flicker of her eyes' image in the dark window. I wonder if they play rougher in their bed, or if it's some demon that mocks me in my dreams and in the glossy prints.

15. I want to get away. I mustn't be here. My dreams are only too predictable. Not of the flesh, no friction of skin and secretion, but camera, action, public spectacle. Me in the centre of the shot and the flashlight behind Joyce's eyes. I wake up. The lights are those of morning. The morning before the last morning – then I'll be gone. Where to? My mother's, back to boyhood temporarily and then at last to my anonymous foreign home.

16. So it's Sunday. Not the lacklustre Sunday that I know – hangover, reading in bed, yawning in the empty town square somewhere between breakfast and tea. Work Sunday, or a Sunday touched by work.

'Give us a hand, will you?'

She shows me how to rake up the straw, pile it into the wheelbarrow and tip it onto the bedding, so long as it isn't too dusty. I'll find something difficult even in a simple job, nervous as I am of failure in the easiest routine – *if it isn't dusty...*

'It's nice to have you here.' Her voice comes from

outside my head, which is absorbed in concepts of duty.
'Are you enjoying yourself?'

'Beautiful countryside.'

'Yes.' She looks around as if I said something novel. 'I'd forgotten that.'

She doesn't go.'You seem,' she says, 'quiet.'

'I'm a quiet person.'

'Only when you want to be.'

As if, as if...

'You're not bored are you? I know we haven't done much to entertain you, but with being so busy...George never rests, you know. All week in the office, then he gets straight down to it on the farm.'

'It's different,' I tell her, 'how can it be boring? I'm glad just not having to think for a while.' My hands nervous, unable to handle the rake and shovel, I lift some of the spiky straw into the wheelbarrow.

'Careful, it's sharp. You need gloves for that.' She shifts from one foot to the other. Her mouth is loose with trouble, appealing perhaps to be kissed. 'We could go for a pub lunch and then swim this afternoon.'

Swimming. Undressing. My thin legs exposed, and the straps around her shoulderblades – 'No no, don't break off your work. I'll go for a walk by myself.'

'Geoffrey,' she insists, 'there isn't that much work.'

I look into the straw that I'm raking.

'No, honestly, there isn't. I do most of it in the week. What George is doing' – helpless – 'well it isn't' – spells out – 'all that necessary. We can spare the time. It's the only holiday I get, when George's friends come.'

'Does George have friends?'

'People from work.' Dismisses. And what of the photographs, Joyce?

'George works everyone into the ground,' she continues. 'He doesn't know how to relax. Sometimes I think he'll never give up his job in London. He doesn't know how to. Even pleasure's hard work to him.'

I scrape harder at the last fragments of straw left on the ground. She stands there, I realise, entirely within my power. For that reason I feel sorry for her.

17. Bells ring out for church – still a social event in the countryside. A priest in purple, tender robes against the rough brick of a building too tiny to hold much of a congregation – the priest says good morning. Everyone says good morning in the countryside. There is no escape. For a while I was lost, the hedgerows so tall I couldn't see where I was. But all roads lead along shallow woods, back to the village. Past the priestly foxgloves, the bitter ferns, towards the place I must, for another morning, call home. No choice. Is that her name? Joyce.

18. 'You'll have to decide,' says George, 'there's the timetable. We'll pass the station on your way back.'

'You're welcome to stay,' says Joyce, meaning more than welcome.

The lunchtime beer had by now sunk right down to my toes. I was sleepy, lying in the half-hearted Sunday sunlight, back to the bumpy pebbles. The slight discomfort seemed to suit me. Suddenly I was feeling doubtful. I might not want to leave after all. I had my reasons.

Joyce undressed coyly behind a towel. I remember stringy net vests with pink round the armholes – Mom taking us on the beach at Blackpool. 'Turn your backs, boys.' Joyce was altogether less substantial, her white legs unnatural fronds against the deep brown of face and arms. I couldn't remember her body as it was in the photographs.

She ran towards the water, white legs flapping like insect wings. 'Come on,' I heard her call. 'It's what we're here for.'

'You must be joking.' George lay flat at my side. 'You wouldn't catch me.'

He closed his eyes. True, it was colder that afternoon, yet the breeze lifted me towards the sea. Beyond the horizon there was France.

I waited for a minute, trying to work out when I could get another look at the photos, just to check. 'What made you do it?' I asked George.

'What?' So contented, so alert, he made a show of being asleep.

'What made you go in for all this?' I watched his closed lids, folded into their sockets, and the curl of his live lips, proclaiming *I am relaxed.* I shall be your executor, I thought. 'You of all people,' I went on, 'you were always interested in machines, not animals or nature – why do you want to be a farmer when you weren't born to it?'

'Property,' he said, 'be your own boss. I can make it work for me here, from start to finish. I can see the results.'

'Is that all?' I said, or perhaps I'd missed the point.

'Listen,' he went on, 'you can't know everything about

everyone. I don't know what you get up to, do I? Or what you want. Or what you really think. Don't want to either. You can't work it out, so be happy with your own life. I'm right, aren't I?'

He opened his eyes on me and then shut them again. I began to think of the spare swimming trunks and the depth of the water, and whether there'd be sand beneath my feet if I waded out. Joyce was standing statue in the shallows, looking out over the waves towards whatever thoughts she had of her own.

'You're getting on well with Joyce,' he said. 'She likes you. You can stay as long as you like, you know. I don't mind.'

That did it. No swimming today.

19. 'If you insist on going – I'll say goodbye.'

'Thank you very much for having me.'

'It was a pleasure. You should've stayed longer.'

'I thought about it, but I did promise Mom…'

'Are you sure there's nothing bothering you? You seem a bit – I don't know – withdrawn.'

She stood in the hallway, so tiny in her bare feet I could've held her in one hand. Her fingers pulled at the locks of hair at the nape of her neck. She was nervous. That was why her eyes were so enormously round.

'It's not your fault, nothing to do with you.' I decided to tell her suddenly. 'There's been something on my mind.'

'Oh.' Eagerness now, to be kind and compassionate and lovable. Behind her head, the book on the shelf was *A Self Help Guide to Therapy.*

'Don't tell George, will you?' No chance of seeing the photographs one last time, to check on the colour of her legs.

She drew closer.

'It's nothing serious – just one of those little incidents. Do you ever look for people you know? In cinemas and railway carriages – do you cast around for a familiar face, even when you know there isn't a chance? This time I did see some one. It wasn't just that I thought for a minute some one's face flashing by was familiar to me. It was real. It was a woman I used to know. She was on the ferry, looking out over the side.'

'Did you speak to her?'

'No. It was the wrong moment. I couldn't break in on her.'

'What did you do?'

'I took her photograph. It's only black and white.'

20. Hannah's lion head. Head of rock. The nose carved so smoothly down to its arches, the mouth set deep and hard, and the eyes, the eyes are marble. Hannah's hair, all grey now, nets the dull day's breeze, and the turned-up collar of her latest cast-off coat catches the channel mist. A sixtieth at f 1.8. She turns at the click of the camera without ever seeing the face behind the lens.

Turn off the taps, unplug the razor, pack the toothbrush. At the bottom of the case, beneath the unworn shirts the unused camera.

Movement to movement. Frame to frame.

'Ready now?' George calls.

Twist the door handle.

'It's open,' he says, 'climb in,'

'She's still asleep?'

'Best not to disturb her. Hard day's work ahead.'

(It's for their own good, she said. They'd only be restless. They'd hurt each other.)

Car door to train door. George trying his best to catch up on the sentiment. 'Take care. Don't do anything I wouldn't do…Give the old girl my love…' He even touches my elbow with his knuckles.

From the window I can see his silver car heading for London, towards nameless hard-earned pleasures. I shan't wind on. The film stays inside the camera, the shutter closed on the twentieth frame.

JUST LIKE ROBERT DE NIRO

This is flesh-and blood me, moving inside the machine. Music's coming up the gutters along Butter Street, Jerusalem Place, Artillery Street, and beyond these shadows the city lights are showing. The streets untangle into junctions, squares and tidal flows; then the orange lamps lead you into Hulme, where there's no sleep, where Michael is, which is Michael.

You get so you don't hear the music any more. Your limbs move of their own accord. I'm stretched thin, strung across the stacked balconies and boarded-up windows and dead lights of Hulme. I'm tired. I liked being tired. At night, I like to feel the pressure of strangers all around me. I'm nowhere. Somewhere they're kicking down doors, the sirens are calling out for some one, everyone's looking out there, among the batteries of people, none of whom is ever Michael.

By day, the concrete's like every rainstorm that ever fell on Manchester, frozen in a grey ice age. They're rocks, the crescents. Look at them – Charles Barry, John Nash, Robert Adam, William Kent, they'll last for ever. They'll outlast any hope of mine, winging its way round the rows of washing, doorways, walkways. I remember two flats boarded up completely, then brown curtains – past another boarded up, I think. But I could be wrong. And they all look like that. The council must be giving out those shit-brown curtains. If I picked the right crescent, if I picked the right storey, the doorways would still be as numerous as the dead.

He said, 'I can't take you in there. It's a fucking shithole,' and slammed the door and walked too fast for me. He stopped, leaned over the edge and said, 'Where do you live then?'

There has to be such a thing as luck. I'll give up on justice, but there has to be such a thing as luck in life. So I come back here every time to look for him at random. Beneath me there's the warm brick red of the Zion Hall, where they filmed the Chicago scenes in *Reds*, and it does look like a film set, too good to be true, glowing vermilion by the pneumonic sixties grey. Diane Keaton trudged through all of Russia looking for Warren Beatty and she found him, she had to. He was hers: he was dying. Michael leaned over the edge, and all we saw was the repetition of the crescents in the rain.

I know this won't be Michael. There's a door bell. But I'll try. I hear movement, rest, then movement again.

'Who is it?' a woman's voice calls, keeping behind those shut brown curtains.

'Excuse me, I'm sorry to disturb you…' When you say the words often enough, you don't hear them any more.

The face is greasy pale, spotty, lovebites on her neck. You can feel the neatness of the flat behind her. You can hear the telly.

'Is he a white guy?'

'Yes, he's about my age, tall, fair hair.' I don't go on adding all the other things he is. It sounds like I'm making him up. 'You can't miss him – very tall, very fair.'

'There's some students on the third floor,' she says doubtfully.

I still can't believe the Aaben's really shut. I thought it was me being insecure when I saw the lager running low, the spirits drained. I always waited for the movies to come to Hulme. I was there every Wednesday, no matter what was showing in the city centre. There was a time when the Aaben advertised in posh papers. There was a time when people brought their cars here, but soon there were only people like me, the holes in their coat linings full of old bus tickets.

I was there, making a fifth or sixth in the seats. Once I thought I was going to be the whole audience. Cameras rolling, action, just for me. I picked the dead-centre seat. I felt like Citizen Kane, until I realised when the lights were low I'd be in just the right spot for a Hitchcock murder. And if I dropped my cigarette packet they'd know it was me.

I loved that place. I sat through a piece on *Monaco-Fairyland by the Sea*, then I waited while they tried to sell me the ultimate jean, Bacardi on the rocks, the bank that likes to say, for the ninety-ninth time – and then there was movement behind me. I could hear fidgeting, coughing, laughter.

The Polish man in a trilby says, 'There's no one like that here. There's some students over the other side.'

'Real students? Or they look like students?'

He gets his keys out, sighs. 'Next time, make sure you get his address.'

Because you can't see through the windows there aren't any clues. People are always kind, but if they aren't Michael they're nothing.

Michael said, 'This place is finished. It's had it. Do you want a stereo? I'll get you one for ten quid. They'll steal anything and sell it for nothing, just to get fucking smack. I'll get you a stereo.'

The more I search, the less I believe in Michael. The young black men laugh and toss their dreadlocks, or they stand suspicious, tight-muscled, trim in doorways. 'Go home. You won't find him.' The young white men are skinned rats, no relation to Michael. They don't answer me at all.

When darkness drops, I go home. There's a hole in my lining, but I've got a real coat with money in the pocket, and I'm scared. I've got a job, a crap job, but Michael's never had a job. I come from that part of Manchester where they still open little cafés and knick-knack shops. I don't need a new stereo. I've got one.

It wasn't a bad film. It was one of those heart-on-your-sleeve social issue movies. There was this grim-faced black detective who'd get to the truth, no matter what. I didn't mind, but it wasn't the kind of film that'd reach out and pull me inside. I could hear every rustle from the person behind me. It was worse than when you bring some one with you and they want to know who's who, and they sit with their arms folded while the tears are starting in your eyes. I could hear the wind racing round the crescents long before the credits were up. I could already feel the rain on my face. I wanted to go.

The other person held the door for me. 'What you think of that then?'

'It was OK. I'll watch anything.'

'Yeah, it was rubbish.'

'Thank God for the Coppola on the telly.'

'Coppola,' he said, like a swear word, and he strode off.

They don't make film stars like Michael any more, so why should he be here in Hulme? They don't even stand the short ones on boxes any more. So what makes me think I'm going to find Michael, with his superhero looks, leaning over a balcony ready to fly, no tricks, no strings, no coke, no heroin. I carry chalk with me to write in the pissy stairwells: I'M LOOKING FOR YOU MICHAEL. That way I can tell where I've already been.

When the phone rings, there's no chance of Michael, so I finish brushing my teeth, I mop my face and replace the towel carefully before I raise the receiver's weight.

I know who it is. It's that other guy Colin, saying do I want to go out for a meal? I don't want to sit still in a restaurant. I want to go out, because I can't stand being locked in. I've got to live. So we'll go dancing.

Michael and me, we like Klaus Kinski, Robert de Niro, Brando. 'You know,' Michael says, 'Robert de Niro goes swimming. He trains his body. That's what I'm doing. I go down Moss Side every morning, twenty lengths at a time, then straight in the gym.

'He wasn't in very good shape in Raging Bull. He was twenty stone.'

'He could do that. He could do what he wanted with his body. He's in control, just like I am.'

There's no phone boxes working in Hulme.

It didn't seem strange the next week to see Michael sitting on the Aaben steps. He said, 'I've got no money. I thought you might buy me a ticket.'

Michael says, 'I don't take drugs. I don't drink. I don't have sugar. Have you got anything to eat at your flat? What is it? I need a high protein diet.' He says, 'I'm getting out of Hulme. I know a girl in the housing department, know what I mean?'

I smoke and I drink. I ride through Hulme in Colin's car. The indicator ticks at the crossroads. I turn the music louder – Baby be good to me – You don't have to cry babe – I'm so sweet to you – till I can hear the songs no more.

Moss Side baths are nearly empty. I can see from the

television screens there's nothing there, just young mums with their kids and some black lads cutting back and forth. When I'm moving through the blue water, I'm shot through light, the pure lights on camera, and I think: this is it, there's no one there, I'm going on for ever and I'll never sleep, night after day, day and night. I can't remember what he looks like any more. All I can see is the clean light of eyes and hair, but they can't be blue. The movie stars wear tinted contact lenses.

The phone's ringing. 'Listen, you're going to have to come to work. You aren't sick. You've been seen out. You're clubbing it.'

When there's a long pause at the end of the line, I know Colin's forgotten to turn the Ansaphone off. The mechanical voice begins: 'Hello. Colin speaking.' I needed him to buy me meals so I had enough money to pay for Michael at the pictures. I can't believe the Aaben's shut. And Michael gone. And it's only half-past nine, it's only eleven, it's two o'clock and I'm not asleep, five o'clock already, August already with no summer to speak of, one week, two weeks already off work. I need Colin's car to take me somewhere.

Television's not the same. Videos only remind you what you felt on the big screen. Bogart says, 'Sober up baby, I'm taking you home.' Trevor Howard leans over the table. He says, 'Shall I see you again?' Brando pours a couple of beers. The phone says, 'If you're not back on Monday, don't bother getting in touch.' The Ansaphone says, 'Hello. Colin speaking.' It'll be morning soon. I can go back to look for him.

I don't even know where I'm going. My legs move of their own accord. I know it's too late now, but I have to keep moving, just to know I'm alive. I'm getting rid of the phone.

They've taken the telly and the video.

They're never anyone playing on the climbing frames and slides. The only kids are travellers' children, barefoot in rags. They brought their caravans right here, where there are endless closed-up flats that no one wants to live in.

The job was crap, but I need money. I can't pay my rent, but I can soon get a council place, if I don't mind moving into Hulme.

Down the dole, everyone looks sick. No wonder he looks rough, standing in his line. I'm tired. My eyes are bad. But I know him. I'd know him anywhere, for the pride in his swimmer's body, bent as it is, the way tall people will hunch when they feel out of place. He knows me too. He looks over to me from out of his dark, demolished face.

In a movie this is where we'd walk over to each other. There'd be close-ups of our smiling faces and the music would play louder. But you can't shoot a movie in a dole office. The lights turn everyone jaundiced. No wonder his face sags. No wonder the Superman blue has gone from his eyes.

One day they'll knock the crescents down. Day by day they board more windows up until entire rows are left vacant. One day Hulme won't be there any more. That'll be the shot, the big one – the crane swinging in the empty sky, then pan down to the rubble below, all of Manchester level at the camera's feet. But there's people in there – numb, nameless people, Michael. There has to be more the silence at the end, in the empty picture house. There has to be more than the sickness in his face.

In the movies, we walked out of line. In the movies, our hands met. We drove out of the city, we flew out of the sky. That's what always happens in the movies.

THE MEMORY ROOM

I can never guess how *Casablanca's* going to end. My memory's wiped from the scene where he says, 'Of all the gin joints in the world...' I want them to be together so badly, Rick and Ilsa. Ilsa, a name so slight it's hardly a murmur, her face half frozen beneath the slanting brim. Am I asking too much? For the moon.

People used to think that soon there'd be no picturehouses. You could get anything you wanted in your own home. It seemed, for a while, as though the world was shrinking. The screens were getting smaller, like the coins and phones and even the spaces we lived in. Then suddenly everybody needed something larger than life. They wanted to lose themselves in the shadows again. And so they rediscovered Hollywood.

But there were only so many stories around. They tried remaking the old movies, but they just weren't the same. There weren't stars any more. Everyone was famous and therefore ordinary. That was where the Memory Room came in.

It's always very quiet in the Memory Room. Stepping through into the curtained space, you find yourself almost in darkness, guided towards the velvety reclining chair. You don't see the equipment. In the corner of your eye, a blue light gleams phosphorescent. You feel a little nip of fear; for half a second – less than that – you want to get out. Then, as the lasers take hold, you catch the dying notes of a piano, the bitter scent of cigarettes, perhaps the sound of breaking glass, and then all those fragments have gone from your brain. You're ready to play it again.

I've seen *Casablanca* maybe a dozen times. Kay was going to *Psycho* every couple of weeks, always opting for the full erasure. When Janet Leigh got into the car, she had no idea where she was heading. When she reached the Bates Motel, she thought, he's a nice boy, nervous, too anxious to please, but basically harmless.

Kay liked to be scared. Some people always take their holidays at the same place, or they order the same dish at their favourite restaurant, or perhaps they always go for a certain type of person. Kay went to see her favourite film over and over. She wasn't the only one. Because of the Memory Room, you could have your cake and eat as much as you wanted, each slice just as fresh as the first.

There were safeguards. What happened to Kay should not have been possible. You can expect some short term disorientation, an inability to focus your eyes, problems finding your transport, but isn't it always like that, when you come out of darkness to light?

So we're in the car with Janet Leigh. Close up, apprehension, she wants to look behind her but she daren't, the eyebrows poised like black gulls, hands clamped to the steering wheel. Kay wants her to get away with the money she stole. It would pay for so very little – a husband, a house and a television set, the simple needs of 1960.

In 1960 you could be locked up for theft. How much more humane we are today. Just a simple modification, and she wouldn't want those things – or not too much. In real life Kay worked in Human Resources. She knew from experience, you have to leave something behind, just a trace of deviance, you'd have to allow her to steal the odd memory stick – no, they didn't have such things – ink and envelopes, whatever they used in those days. You make way for some minor transgressions, or else the brain simply implodes.

Just as she draws up at the motel, Kay feels a gentle seepage in her stomach. Something's wrong. She's not quite well. She moves quickly down the aisle, towards the facilities. The audience is small tonight, perhaps on account of the weather. People are afraid of sudden change. It could warm up again, or worsen, no point in trying to forecast.

Inside the cubicle, a splash of blood drops onto the white marble floor. She sits terrified on the toilet; could she be bleeding to death? It shines like a red penny against the sheer white marble. She sits, she sits trying to stem the panic. She must be menstruating – no, surely not – but what else can it be? Nanna used to go on about menstruation and menopause, the change and the curse; how once you had to wear some kind of cotton wadding inside yourself, and you had to lie down for days at a time, and you went through irrational phases that could even lead to violence. Kay's had the treatment like everyone else. No one menstruates these days. It's disgusting. Primitive. Like childbirth. They used to do that too; she's seen it in the movies.

The panic starts to well, but she knows what to do – go underground to the old folk. They know how to deal with such things. Kay swills the blood down the drain – the blood from her knickers – then holds them up to the instant dry. The cubicle scents, hyacinths and freeze-dry roses, are overwhelmingly sweet. Glancing at her face in the mirror above, she sees hollows under her eyes, shadows cast by the bleached lighting of the miniature white palace.

No point wasting time in the Memory Room. She can get herself sorted next week; she hasn't seen enough of the film to need full re-adjustment. Right now, she wants transport. She hurries through the moonlit gardens, through the rustling trees and the squeaking of owls, icy rain prickling at her face. She's searching for the subway, but there's something else at the back of her mind – something she's left behind, or maybe something unfinished at work.

She finds the subway entrance where it always is, at the far side of the Picture House, which is sparkling like a crystal, sending heat into the night. And there's a child sliding down the banister, a genuine child like she used to be, in a little hooded jacket; she's never seen one so close, not since she became an adult. She wants to see its face, but she can't on account of the hood. She ought really to do something; that child is valuable. But there's no time, and besides, it serves them right, whoever mislaid it – their own fault for being so careless.

A subway car's pulling up at the foot of the stairs. Before she can remember what that nagging thing might be, she's on her way towards the granny shops.

It's far too hot down here. She hates being among the numberless old, pressed together underground where they have their own comforts, their muddled stores and drinking places, where they're allowed to smoke and prepare meals in their own laborious manner. They're quite happy. All the same, it's depressing to watch. How long since she saw Nanna? A half-memory trickles through her mind. Her old woman's skin was like chalk; you could rub her away. She said, come to Nanna, don't be shy, I won't hurt you. Sitting in a rocking chair, bony ankles in big slippers. She wanted to steal me. Steal me away.

Kay's much better now. She surreptitiously feels herself, examining a pinkish film on her fingertips that might be no more than the iridescence of moist flesh. It's just the heat, that's all, the heat in this buried place. Reaching over, in the empty cab, to reset her direction, she glimpses a gaunt face in the window, reflected against the fathomless walls of the shaft – a stranger, herself in the dark. She looks like some one who ought to be asleep.

Soon she's back overground, speeding through the spacious city towards the corporate settlement where she has lived ever since she left school. The snow's coming down so fast, she can't tell which route she's taking. But it doesn't really matter. Everything's under control. At home she changes her soiled clothes and cleans herself. The bleeding's stopped completely. Even the stains are much fainter than she imagined.

Tonight there are no messages. Nothing she has left to do. So she sits quietly, enjoying the hundred square metres granted to a minor employee at Human Resources. It's a long time she's sat as still as this without watching or waiting, all by herself. When the lights go out at midnight, the whole room's silvered by the shimmering snow. If she'd stayed in the movie, she'd have missed all of this. She'd have gone straight to bed, probably. She falls asleep, listening to the switched-off silence, all traces of the day fading into something less than afterthought.

In the morning, the snow was still there, a dense woollen weight, smothering the fields beyond the settlement. Earth and sky merged into one another. Nothing seemed to move. Kay stood mesmerised, watching a single gull drifting against the pale landscape like a scrap of fuselage.

That was how I found her, gazing out of the window, as if lost in her own thoughts. 'There's something wrong with my eyes,' she said. 'I'm colour blind.'

I didn't know what she meant.

'I can't see any colours.'

Of course she couldn't, not on this winter's day, overlooking the snow, and with all her equipment down. I went to turn her monitor back on, to show the multicoloured screensaver springing back to life. But it was no good. She wouldn't leave the window. She wasn't listening to me. I don't think she knew who I was. I can't even be sure she saw the gull, or anything beyond her own reflection.

No one ever stays away from Human Resources. No one's ever late – or if they are, if that's their designated weakness, they still remain in contact. They don't switch themselves off. As Kay's superior, I felt responsible. And she was a beautiful woman, a classic like Dietrich or Garbo, with a body geometrically perfect, a face carved out of ice. That morning we were completely alone; I could have touched her. I might have broken all the rules, if she hadn't started to tell me her story.

I still plan to use the Memory Room, despite what happened to Kay. She was unstable. We – that is, the Management – deliberately made her that way, genetically designed to belong to that small minority which is susceptible to sensory overload. A sad story, but quite exceptional, a collision of circumstances – the supposed menstruation, linked with delusions concerning an alleged grandmother. A pity, but what can you do? When I left, I was tempted to look back, to see if

137

she was still there, standing at the window in her Queen Christina pose. But you should never turn round. You should always look ahead. Tomorrow, so they tell us, is another day, and one more forgotten ending waiting to unravel in the twilight.

NOVEMBER

To Paul, God Bless – Be a Good Boy Now – Goodnight Paul —
He always takes the best.

Sefton Park. 'A magnificent achievement of mid-Victorian suburban planning and municipal enterprise.' Two hundred and sixty-nine acres, the largest outdoor space since Regents Park. Designed by Lewis Hornblower and the Frenchman Edouard André, its sweeping boulevards recall the Bois de Boulogne, whose development André oversaw a few years previously, when he was chief gardener to the city of Paris.

Easy to get lost in Sefton Park. Inside, you'll find the landscape gently dips, leading you further into its heartland, guided by the little brooks running down towards the lake. Soon you lose sight of the traffic edging along the perimeter, though in fact the roads are never far away. The trees seem ancient – massive oaks and chestnuts and groves of weeping willow. You forget this is not a real forest. It's manmade.

November. The last flush of brightness before darkness covers the earth. The leaves ablaze in alchemical shades, bronze, gold and sulphur. *And the Glory of the Lord shall be revealed.* November 2004. The Battle of Falluja. Bombings, beheadings, the slitting of throats. A fall in house prices predicted. Everton has made a flying start to the season, standing at third place in the premier league.

Football mad he was football mad from the minute he could walk true blue born and bred you should have seen him kick a ball.

November, the month of *The Messiah*. *But who may abide the day of his coming, and who shall stand when he appeareth? For he is like a refiner's fire.* On Halloween a lantern procession troops through the park, paper shades glowing pale in the darkness. As the fireworks hit the sky, a monstrous figure flames above the lake like something out of *Quatermass*. A gigantic wicker man, twisting and turning, changing shape as the lanterns are tossed in the water, *and the trumpet shall sound and the dead shall be raised incorruptible.*

The Palm House (1896, restored 2001) is an octagonal domed structure, built from iron and glass. It rests on a plinth of polished red granite, sporting bronze or marble statues at each of its eight angles. The statues represent le Notre, Cook, Mercator, Linnaeus, Darwin, Columbus, Henry the Navigator and the physician John Parkinson – inspirational figures, representing science and exploration.

Every day I walk my dog in Sefton Park, entering at Lark Lane and making for the Palm House, then looping round William Rathbone's statue, crossing the stepping stones over the brook and heading back to Lark Lane via the disused fountain by the café. Just below the glistening spider of the Palm House, where the path forks down towards the white and greenish worthy gazing out across the lake – up towards a meadow, backlit by winter sunshine – I pass a great beech tree.

140

Without even seeing that it is a beech But today this one tree stands out from the rest, a startling splash of paintbox colours – scarlet, yellow and bright purple, oranges and creamy whites. Its trunk is parcelled in red ribbon, and bunches of flowers have been laid at the foot. If you come close, you can see where the bark has been gashed. A line of white dashes, like stitches in the tarmac, tracks an arc towards the point of impact.

Over the next few days, more bouquets arrive, covering the bank with lilac cellophane. Or tied to the tree with cards and photographs. *Miss your cheeky face.* His name is Paul, and this Paul can be no other than the Paul Stephen Lamkin whose death notice appears in the *Echo* on Friday November 19th, *tragically aged 23 years*, and whose cremation is handled by Charletts Funeral Services Lark Lane, where *Paul will be resting*. But some call him Muscles, and one picture shows him standing in his bedroom flexing his arms like a champion.

My wonderful son so young and beautiful. Why have you gone away.

People stop to puzzle, and slowly word gets round. Three young lads in a Honda Civic at three o'clock in the morning. One's dead, one's broke his neck, the other's facing charges. So they say. The park's a sociable place. The dog walkers nod to each other, sometimes lingering for a chat while their pets romp and tussle. *Beautiful morning. Makes you glad to be alive.* And so we are. A toddler staggers by the duckpond, its mother pushing the buggy a few steps behind, and a pair of cyclists skim past.

Two little dicky birds sitting on a wall.

After a few days, the funeral wreaths appear – the letters SON spelt out in flowers; a lucky horseshoe; red Liver Bird against a white shield; a football, like a birthday cake, in flowers instead of icing. *I can't believe this has happened – He always takes the best – Who am I going to do murder with now?*

One named Peter, one named Paul.

Three of them. So the story goes. Racing round the park just for the hell of it, swerving round the bends like Monte Carlo. *Bloody menace. They get what's coming. Good riddance. Bleeding scallies.* Hard words said out loud. But most of the regulars skirt that section of path, averting their eyes from the shrine. Only the weekend strollers stop to wonder, pausing hand-in-hand to read the floral tributes. There are other stories, other deaths, and on the far side of the park there's another memorial.

People keep putting flowers on the tree, but we can't expect that to go on forever.

November 2000. Four years already since Jennifer died. Since then there have been further incidents – children struck down as they're crossing the road, pensioners knocked spinning into the next world. But this death, neither more nor less dreadful, remains the most starkly dramatic; and in its cruel ironies stands for the rest. *I still ask why. But there's no answer, is there, or none that's given to us. Not in this life.* Lucy, lucky Lucy the survivor, stands next to Jen's parents and her brother, people she barely knew before November 96. She has become a substitute daughter. Jen's mother still writes letters, the only person left who still writes letters.

So we thought something permanent, a bench in the park, somewhere people can sit down and rest, we think she might like that, give something back to the people of Liverpool, because they were so kind weren't they, after it happened, so generous, and she loved this place.

Getting back on her feet, after the press photograph, Lucy feels suddenly dizzy. That's the way grief comes to her now, in turns and panics, dropped cups and lost keys, a pain behind the eyes, the last traces of her injuries. She grips the bench, her fingers clasping the cold metal plaque.

Remembering the good times, until we meet again.

Kids messing round with a ouija board. On a winter's night, sitting in a circle, staring at the glass. *Is anybody there?* You get the giggles and are shushed and then suddenly feel scared. The others seem different, solemn and sober, no longer themselves. *Stop*, you want to say, *stop it you, I know it's you, stop pushing the glass* and yet you daren't. You're all fascinated. You have yet to lose anyone from your generation. You haven't yet encountered death.

You fumble with your laces. Jen's by the door, jigging with impatience. *Come on Luce, get your arse in gear.* You have to force yourself sometimes. Especially when it's raining. The winds are fierce round here, shearing off the Irish sea. But once you've made the effort you feel so much clearer somehow, clearer in your head, and your feet seem to fly.

Still missing you loads. Hope you're dancing with the angels.

Like when the plane leaves the ground. That one moment of fear, then your heart seems to lift and you're way above ground. Or when the music starts, that special song your body knows. Or a ball sailing through the stratosphere, crossing midfield and heading straight for the net.

November 1996. The Rwandan massacres spread into Zaire. Guns, amputations, human shields. Further revelations following the royal divorce. Everton thrash the Saints 7-1, scoring a goal within the first minute. *Prepare ye the way of the Lord, make straight in the desert a highway for our God.*

Five thirty on Thursday, fifteenth of November. Just time for a short run, and then a shower and something to eat. They're feeling good as they enter the park from the Halls of Residence. And so is the killer speeding towards them in a stolen Astra, with a handbag on the seat that he's nicked from some woman loading up at Tesco. Luck is on his side as he cuts through the rush hour, shooting through the lights, hardly touching the parked cars and the stationary traffic. Nothing can touch him. It's like being invisible, blasting at warp speed across the universe.

Rain prickling the skin. Sirens whooping, as always at this hour in the city, hark the children of the night. Heart beating, limbs keeping pace automatically. Jen grins at Luce – *see, not so bad?*

And then, and then...

The girls didn't stand a chance. That car wasn't driving, it was flying.

Perhaps he didn't see them. Perhaps he saw nothing except a smear of bright lights; heard nothing but the engine's roar as he put his foot down harder. Blind instinct funnelled him towards the park like a fox going to ground. He thought nothing, felt barely a judder as he bumped against what might have been the branches of a tree Afterwards there would have been no escape from knowing.

Young Doc killed by Hit-Run Yob: Pal Lucy Fights for Life. Mother Pleads: Give Yourself Up. We Know It Was An Accident.

She was everyone's dream daughter, and he was scum, right? If you can weigh one life against another, the scally against the medical student, are the scales equally balanced? Beautiful, the papers called her, brilliant. But he was bound for hell. He torched the Astra and found himself another vehicle, the car in which he would shortly be obliterated. He died in a police chase, a few days later. That didn't bring the girl back. Nothing can.

See you when I get there.

When your number's up, you're done for. Nothing you can do.

Still think I see you walk into Dom 1's.

St. George's Hall (begun 1841, completed 1854) stands on an elevated plateau close to Lime Street Station. Its young architect, Harvey Lonsdale Elmes, combined classical grandeur with a boldly innovative vision. The inscription over the southern portico, *Artibus, Legibus, Consiliis*, affirms the civic values behind this ambitious project, funded entirely by public subscription. After Elmes's early death, construction was largely supervised by C.R. Cockerell, who was responsible for the richly decorative interior. The ornate brass doors leading to the concert hall incorporate the letters SPQL (the Senate and the People of Liverpool). The huge organ stands at the north end, mounted on a circular platform, its pipes supported on the shoulders of sea giants.

Whenever I look at St. George's, I'm awestruck and amazed, its stone flanks reminding me yet again of some prehistoric monument, a sacrificial temple or a sealed tomb. Another race lived here and might return, Cthulhu submerged by the estuary, a mile or so away. A people more durable than human beings, less easily damaged.

At little more than half a century, I count myself amongst the younger members of the audience. Glancing round at the balding heads, hunched shoulders and over-sized spectacles, I feel almost girlish in comparison. The choir stands ranked before us, silent as the nameless dead, while the soprano climbs, note by note, towards the immortal realms. But in which flesh exactly shall we see God? Surely not the weathered carcasses we wore when we were living. Thirty, was it St Augustine who said we'd all be thirty?

And the trumpet shall sound... The bass voice intervenes, rebounding against the trumpet solo, repeating those words and those notes on and on with increasing momentum until you're almost sick of it but you're not, you want the ride to go on for ever. And I feel such pure joy, the joy the dogs feel running through the park.

Sometimes in winter the trees seem alive. The spirits of the dead inhabit them. In sorrow you might wrap your arms around a tree, embracing its torso like a human body. The funeral tributes have been cleared from the foot of the beech tree. The wire framework spelling out the letters SON rests against a railing next to a bin bag. The bunches of flowers have lasted longer than you might expect, preserved by the cold and wet, although the ink on the cards has nearly dissolved. And the ribbon's still there, wrapped like a tourniquet round the trunk. Another photograph is tucked inside, Paul and his mate framed by a car window, or maybe a coach – yes, they're ready for the off, looking pleased with themselves, grinning straight at the camera. Cheers pal. Nice one. See you later.

THE REAL LOUISE

On the far side of the park, Louise will be bidding her parents goodnight, closing the door softly, with a gentle sigh of relief. Settling on the spare bed, she'll soak up the silence at the end of the day, listening for the shush of rain in the trees before picking up something to read. Closer, closer, he can smell her now, hear the click of the light switch – does she talk in her sleep? He needs her so urgently that, without even thinking, he's tapping the L and the O, dialling the direct line to his heart, if not to his head.

'He came over to our table and he says to your dad, "Is there any other reason you've not been coming? She looks well enough to me." Called him to one side and said is there another reason? Well you know your dad. He was fuming. He said, "Excuse me, Bob, excuse me..."'

Louise is faintly conscious of a bell shrilling somewhere, as she's faintly conscious of everything right now – her mother patting the cups with a tea towel, the babbling of the telly in the knock-through lounge.

'What I think it is, we pick this other lady up and if we don't go she has to stay at home. We never missed the club before, just that one week and he comes straight up and says is there another reason...'

Her dad's materialised, brandishing the silver mobile, pleased with himself for mastering the alien implement. 'It's Chris,' he says abruptly, turning back towards *Big Brother.*

Chris? Do I know any Chris?

Louise is a traveller. She has never settled down, never had children, or kept the same job for more than a year. And those itchy feet are both the reason for her solitude and her escape. No sooner is she back from one trip than she's planning another, searching for those destinations where myths begin and end, far shores and mountain summits that can only be attained through hardship and perseverance. To Chris, they're just names. Ladakh – Samarkand – Timbuktu – they might as well be El Dorado, Shangri-la. How can they be real places, with shops and bus stations? When she gets out her photos he doesn't really believe that these wide streets and shop signs are the actual Katmandu or that those barren ranges are the Himalayas as he remembers them from Kipling.

What Chris sees is not so much the changing backdrop as the travelling companions. 'That's Martin,' she'll say, or 'there's Pete – there's Pete again...' on every expedition there's a Pete or a Martin or Dave who stands out from the rest, rangy and confident, pedalling his bike round a mountain pass or striding along a ravine. The cyclists all look identical in their helmets, like a swarm of androgynous elves. Louise herself is barely distinguishable from this Pete or Martin, who is sometimes the official tour guide or sometimes an especially well informed amateur she's palled up with for the duration.

He has no right to be jealous. He tells himself, in any case, these people are not into sex. They're into mind fucks, enraptured and exhausted like medieval saints. She comes back from those faraway kingdoms, lean and ragged, her brown legs bruised, her thoughts elsewhere. Of all the women he's known she's probably the least sexual. Sex for her is just an appetite; she's not much interested in food, either – snacks on crisps and apples. Keeping it simple suits him fine – or it did.

So what made him so angry this time? Maybe it was reading about that poor guy on his way up Everest – or ' Eve Rest' as we should say, that was how the eponymous Colonel Sir George pronounced the name. He heard that on the radio, remembered it for her. At a certain altitude, you become euphoric, believe yourself immortal. And, gripped by this delusion, the guy simply threw away his mask. What got to Chris was the way that other walkers passed him by. 'How could you do that?' he said. 'How could you just keep going?'

'What would be the point? There was nothing they could do.'

'Even so, even if you knew that, if you were one hundred per cent, how could you let a man die alone?'

'It's not like that. You don't understand. In that situation you have to save yourself.'

'There's parties going up there – paying thousands of pounds – to prove what?' And he could suddenly see Louise herself amongst the horde, shrugging as she trekked onwards through the snow. 'It's just tourism. I bet you there's people been up Everest who'd never dare go into the centre of Liverpool on a race day. They have to cross the planet to prove they're so bloody superior.'

She got out of bed and put her dressing gown on.

'I don't mean you,' he added.

'You'll be late,' said Louise. Against the white gown, her skin was terracotta. 'You'd better make a move.'

'I'll call you,' he said when he'd showered.

'My parents are coming tomorrow. They'll be here all week.'

'When they've gone....'

'Yeah.' Her whole attitude showed utter boredom and disdain. When he grabbed hold to say goodbye she said, 'Oh fuck off, can't you? You don't even want to be here. You despise people like me, yeah, 'cause you're such a fucking coward in your own life.'

'What can I do? I apologise. I'm glad you had a good time. Really.'

'Fuck off. And don't come back.'

'Louise. Don't be like that.' He held her close. She didn't struggle. 'Have a nice time with your parents. I'll see you the week after next.'

Minutes afterwards he wondered why he didn't do something, why he just meekly drove home with his love left unsaid. Force of habit. Like his marriage. That one week dragged more slowly than the six she'd been away. Until finally he could stand it no longer.

'Hi Chris,' she says sounding – not angry at least, more sort of bemused.

'They're still there then.'

'Yes.'

'And are they enjoying their visit?'

'Well yeah – we went to the Palm House – and over to Formby – they're just happy to be here...' She lowers her voice, wandering, he imagines, round the flat, finding a corner to speak in '....wish I had their energy... Dad's been putting shelves up, she insists on washing up. You wouldn't think there was anything wrong with her – no, that's not right – you can tell, of course you can tell. If you know.'

151

She goes on talking about her mother's diagnosis, something he's grown used to as a GP, friends appealing to his judgement apologetically. But not Louise, who always seems unfettered by family worries. This is another Louise, moving closer to him, drawing him inside her deeper concerns. He says the usual reassuring things. She says, as they all do, 'I feel so helpless... I mean what can I do, I can't be down there.... Anyway, how are you?'

'Me, I'm fine, great.' He is not.

Great? He says the word like a Scouser, growling, almost purring.

'Chris?' she says.

'Hmm?'

'Chris? Why did you ring?'

'I'm sorry Louise, with your parents and all – I couldn't leave things as they were – I don't know what to say ....'

He's still talking, a wave of speech, the Scouse cadences rising and falling, and the voice is obviously not her old friend from back home, how could she for a second have thought that it was, but she knows him from somewhere, she's sure about that, he has a kind voice or else she'd have put down the phone.

At last she says, 'I think you've got the wrong Louise.'

The wrong Louise. He thinks for a minute that she's speaking metaphorically. And then she says, 'Do I know you?'

The *Big Brother* theme belts out from the living room. And that something familiar slides into place.

'Aren't you Lynn's husband?' she says.

He doesn't remember her at all, this other Louise.

'You rang me, didn't you, when she had the flu ....we were doing *The Kite Runner*....and you picked her up once or twice....We have met. Sorry Chris, it is Chris isn't it....I thought something was wrong but I couldn't put my finger on it ...'

She won't tell, this other Louise. He wishes she would, but she'll shelve it away none of her business. And yet this is it, the moment that will change his life forever, when he decides to pack up and leave everything behind him.

A light's shining under the bedroom door. His wife's reading *The Good Soldier* by Ford Madox Ford; they do classics sometimes in the book group. She can't really get into it, but she's persevering. He prefers non-fiction – biographies and travel books – *Maximum City, The Road to Oxiana*. Usually they both read till one switches their light off, and then the other – 'Good night love' – she still calls him 'love'. 'Sleep well.' And they sleep side by side till morning comes and they each go their separate ways.

BE A GOOD GIRL

Sundays were the long days at Grandma's. Every quarter of an hour the clock would chime the first laborious notes in an endless sequence. The clock was dark and massive like the huge gothic dresser and the piano that nobody played. Sun and Moon smiled at me from the tall clock, but that was a grandfather clock and Grandad was dead.

I wasn't allowed down from the stiff-backed chairs until everyone had finished. So I kept my eyes on the china shepherdesses and dogs caught on the many high ledges. In summer, the dust was trapped by sunlight freckled through the crumbly lace curtains. Everything smelt of mothballs. When I couldn't eat I'd sit waiting for the spidery fingers to edge along V, X, I. There was no proper time on the clock, only V, X, I. There was no television, no wireless, no one to play with. If I had my new bouncy beachball I'd send it as high as the real moon and sun. *The little dog laughed...*but since I couldn't run, I sat.

I watched the patterns in the parched crockery, on the yellowed wallpaper, on the stitched antimacassars and doilies. There was a lady, Mary Mary, her face covered by a poke bonnet amongst the lupins on the firescreen. The copper kettle cast the shadow of a long-necked beast. Many islands were mapped on the dark red carpet; there were plenty of secrets in that chill, airless room.

Whenever I went to Grandma's, I wore my best frock, the one Grandma bought for my latest birthday. There were always layers of nylon caught at the waist, sometimes pink, sometimes powder blue. It was the dress I was wearing in the framed photograph on the dresser, the only colour picture, standing in between the wedding and the army photos.

As Mummy jerked my hair into an elastic band, she'd say, 'Now have you been? Are you sure you've been? You'd best go again to be on the safe side. Now try and keep yourself nice,' she'd say, pulling the hem of my coat straight. 'Don't forget to say thankyou,' she'd say, twisting round from the front seat of the car. You'd scarcely know it was Mummy on Sundays. Her lips were glazed with red, her figure squeezed inside a tight-fitting suit.

As we walked through the gate she'd still be brushing loose threads and dandelion wings from my shoulders. But once we were inside all the grown-ups ignored me.

They were all sat round the table – Auntie Violet, Auntie Florence, Auntie Gertrude; and then the next generation, Peggy, Betty, Marge, by the side of their silent other halves.

A voice would clatter with the cutlery. 'This weather doesn't suit me. The sun gives me a shocking headache.'

Or, if it was raining, the conversation was rheumatics. Some one would get up to close the curtains or shut a door against the draught.

It was during one of these drawn-out moments, as a chair creaked and feet padded, that I felt my bladder start to expand as slowly, as distinctly, as a voice inside me.

'Mummy...'

Mummy was sipping the thin soup thoughtfully. She seemed not to hear me. 'Mummy, Mummy...' I touched her sleeve. 'Mummy, I want to go.'

She shushed me, looking round without turning her head. 'You'll have to hold it till we get home.'

'I can't. I feel bad.' My voice was rising. Still no one

looked at me. 'I feel poorly, Mum.'

'Be a good girl. Just behave yourself till we get home,' she hissed. 'Haven't I told you, you can't go round people's houses asking to use the toilet.'

The soup bowls were cleared and the plates handed round – cold, fatty lamb with three boiled potatoes, one and a half for the child.

'Eat a little bit. Just try, there's a good girl. Grandma goes to a lot of trouble.'

I tried to eat, because the horrible feeling of eating would be worse than the other horrible feeling. If I ate all the fat, Grandma would fetch out a boiled sweet from the bottom of her musty handbag. But instead of making me forget, the food made me feel worse, as if my whole body was bursting. I thought of the seven times table, which was always trickier than the sixth; then the divide by, harder than times; and in pounds, shillings and pence. Then I thought hard about the nastiest things I could remember, like the big girl who waited outside school sometimes, or chickenpox, or the dead cat with flies in its gums. These thoughts took me from II to XI, from pale brussel sprouts to watery trifle. But there was still washing up to go, cups of tea, whist, the drive home.

Mummy was in the kitchen washing up. I tugged at her pinny but her back wouldn't turn.

One of the old trembly aunts patted my head. 'Aren't you a big girl now! And how are you enjoying school?'

'I want to go,' I said in a small voice.

The aunt continued in her loud voice: 'And are you a good girl for the teachers, Marietta? That's nice!' She had a pink tube in her ear. Another auntie couldn't eat cake, it was too rich for her digestion. Another gave me half crowns in sealed envelopes.

I went to the bottom of the stairs and looked up into the secret core of the house. No one would know if I slipped up to the toilet. But I couldn't. It was dark. Grandma slept there, and I was scared of Grandma. There were hairs on her face. She smelt all dusty.

I sat on the steps, my face deep in my nylon skirts.

When we got home, Mummy would run into the house, stumbling over the Yorkshire terrier. 'This girdle's killing me.' She'd kick off her high heels, fall into a chair and call out: 'Did you hear her showing off about that motor? It's all on tick, you know. They've no money of their own. They're all show. I don't know why she married him. He's common as muck. She could have had her pick when she still had her figure...Four doors! I know damn well they only make them with two...'

She'd pull me to her sharply, to get the buttons and ribbons undone. When the ice cream van tinkled in the street she'd say, 'Alright then, just a small one, for being a good girl,' and I'd skip outside with twopence in my hand.

'Watch the traffic!' she'd shout, and then resume in a low, adult's voice: 'It's about time somebody did something with Auntie Violet. Did you see her with the peas?'

With my eyes shut, I could've been anywhere. The nylon was sand on my cheeks. The skirts rustled like the seashore. It was easy to pretend. The anger would break on me soon, but not now, later. I need not think about it now. I could enjoy the wet warmth pulsing through my knickers. Then I heard distant chimes moving into sequence, slowly at first and then with insistence. I'd never look at Sun and Moon again.

THE TELEPHONE RINGING, THE KNOCK AT THE DOOR

Judith's Office

If Judith was married, this wouldn't be happening. She's not the only child. She's not even the favourite. But the other two are left in peace; they belong to other people.

She tries to explain. 'Look Mum, I'm at work. I've got some one waiting. I'll ring you back, okay?'

The student's slouched forward in the low vinyl chair, his two wings of hair drooped over his specs. He's not the very worst, but suddenly she hates him. If he was a spider, she'd tread on him now.

'You can't have another deadline, not without a doctor's note. Anyway, what's happened to you? I've not seen you this semester.'

'I've been having problems.' His voice so low, she can hardly catch a word he's saying.

'What kind of problems?'

'Personal problems.'

Yes, like getting out of bed in the morning. Judith was no different thirty years ago.

'Well.' He screws up his half-asleep eyes. 'It's like, my parents have moved house.'

'You live with your parents?'

'No.'

The course leader appears at the door, beckoning. 'I'm sorry Judith,' he says between his teeth, 'but Claire Gordon swears she handed in that first assignment.'

She's certain, she's convinced, she hasn't had the essay. But there's always a corner for doubt in her mind. By the time she's searched through every pile of dead paper, the lecture plans, research notes, agendas, notices, reading lists, timetables, that cover every surface; by the time she's explored the dusty recesses of her filing cabinet and emptied drawers of Bluetac, envelopes, herbal teabags, aspirin, floppy disks and paperclips, another half a dozen students have gathered like enervated moths around the door. Judith wanted to get home early today. She has a paper to finish, 'Being and Becoming in Contemporary Spanish Film'.

Oh fuck, she thinks to herself in the car, fuck fuck. I never rung her back. I'd best go straight over. What is it this time? Her library books need changing? The binmen spilt some rubbish? TV's untuned itself?

Half a dozen DVDs clatter to the floor as she grabs a muesli bar from the glove compartment. She remembered to bring a sandwich this morning but she forgot where she put it. Now she's driving out of the city towards a place where the sky presses down on the hills like a lid.

Shit, I'll have to stay for my tea now. All that cake she makes me eat, she thinks sugar gives you energy. Shit shit shit shit. At least today she got the message. She didn't keep on ringing, once I told her, that was it.

When Judith reaches Victory Row she finds out why. Her mother's fallen downstairs, running from the toilet to answer the phone. She's been lying there helpless for hours, her knickers still round her knees – those saggy white drawers that have seen better days.

'I went flying,' Vera says. 'Eh Julie, you should've heard

159

the thump.'

There's only one person who calls her by that name. Judith's mother, who is five stone overweight. Who is troubled by asthma and strange palpitations, who sometimes rings her up because she heard things in the night. She's already had one heart attack. She needs to be looked after. She shouldn't be alone.

Carol's house is too small. Plenty of room at Pam's, but Mum and Brian can't stand each other. But Judith has space, now that she's split up with Peter. If Mum sells her house there'll be enough to buy his share and fit a downstairs toilet too, maybe an extension. She could have the upstairs, her mother the ground floor. It wouldn't be so bad. She could live with it. She'd have to. Better than rushing back and forth.

It seems so obvious.

Two bed mid-terrace. Enclosed yard to rear. Requires updating. Convenient location.

Vera's House

People march in, no wiping their feet, half an hour early, why do they have to always come when you're sitting down to eat?

'See,' Vera says, slamming the drawers shut, 'you've got all your cupboards. I'm leaving the carpets, that's all thrown in. They're good carpets, they've lasted me years. I suppose you want to see the bedrooms.'

She lumbers upstairs, wheezing badly. Any more of this, and she'll be after another turn. The young couple are more or less babies. They hold hands, squinting nervously, her in a little girl's dress with great clod-hopping shoes; him lanky, sober-faced, scribbling in a black book.

They're not keen. After close to a year at this game, she can tell. 'How lovely,' the girl chirrups. 'How nice, oh beautiful!' She raves over the fish tank as if she's never seen one in her life. The lad peers at the pipes underneath the wash basin. You have to show them everything, even your toilet. These strangers, barging into your home, taking it all it.

'Half an hour to heat the water. Enough to fill a bath.'

'You haven't got a combi-boiler?'

What's a combi-boiler? Vera presses on regardless. 'You've a timer. Just set it to come on and you can have a bath when you come home.'

Ten minutes and they've seen everything there is to see. Oh well. At least the tea's still warm in the pot. When they've gone she can cut herself another slice of angel cake.

'Can we ask,' the lad enquires, not much older than Pam's eldest, 'why it is you're moving?'

She hesitates. 'Family reasons.'

What's it to do with them?

'Oh well,' Judith sighs when she tells her all about it. 'Don't give up. Nine months is nothing these days.'

'We should change the estate agent. Next door but one's sold.'

'Yes, but look at the work they've had done.'

'What's wrong with this house? It's been looked after.'

'No double glazing, for a start.'

'Waste of money. This house was built to last. It doesn't need anything doing, just a lick of paint, that's all. I'm seventy-eight years old. You can't expect me to go climbing up ladders.'

Julie's hardly touched that piece of haddock. The only nourishment she ever gets is what she's given here. Won't eat meat. No sugar in her tea. Pale and skinny, all dressed in black, the ghost of Christmas yet to come. Vera scrapes the leftovers onto her plate. If there's anything she can't abide, it's waste.

'I don't know why you can't come home. They're all moving out here from Manchester. You don't get mugged round here. I don't know what you've got against it. I thought you liked the countryside. The station's down the road, if you don't want to drive to work.'

'We've talked about this already.'

No they haven't. Vera's mentioned it, and Julie's changed the subject. She can be a bit funny, our Julie. She's not like her sisters. She'll never confide. Vera knows better than to ask what happened to that chap of hers, the one she was living with. She remembers saying once to Julie, 'This Peter, is he black?'

And Julie snapping at her, 'Why, what's it to you?'

'I'm only asking.' Because, she wanted to say, if that's the reason I've not met him, I don't mind.

Snarling back at her, the image of her dad. Yet she's never laid eyes on the bugger since she was six months old. You'd have thought nature would have left something of Vera inside her own daughter.

'I've got some carrot cake in the fridge,' Vera says, 'have you tried carrot cake? Carol fetched me it from Sainsbury's.'

'None for me, thanks, I'm full up.'

'Go on, be a devil.' Vera leans across the table, eyes glinting wickedly. 'Just this once won't harm you. Have a little slice, for me.'

The Bedroom

Pink. Blush pink, cherry blossom, the colour of pink medicine. Candyfloss. Not hot pink, not shocking pink either. Coconut ice or school blancmange. The whole room's flushed with a rich, fleshy glow. Trellised wallpaper: rose bouquets tied by fluttering pink ribbons. One single bed – the other has been shifted downstairs for Vera, leaving a vivid rectangle on the fitted carpet.

A pink and white plastic tray, embossed with rosebuds, arranged on the dressing table between matching powder bowls. All three resting on crocheted mats. On the tray, a perfume spray, a comb and hairbrush, also with a rose motif. The drawers are empty except for the lining paper and a couple of hair grips.

A quarter past nine. At home, the evening's just begun, but here she's as ready for bed as her mother. Children's voices drift up from the street. If you push the nets aside and poke your head out of the window, you can just make out the hills, beyond the plastics factory. Two balsa-framed pictures are stuck on the wall, one showing a curly-haired infant kissing a budgie, the other another child scolding a St Bernard. Two apple-cheeked little girls.

This room belonged to Pam and Carol. Julie shared a bed with her mother while she waited for her sisters to get married. But neither of them did till she was leaving anyway, already on the verge of being Judith.

Now Judith sleeps here twice a week, sometimes three times. She lies between the nylon sheets, pulling at candlewick, thinking, if we were in a play there'd be a big scene and I'd say, you never loved me. You only had me to try and keep my dad. Pity I wasn't a boy. Everything else would come out, all of it, then they'd make up, or else Judith would stomp out, I'm leaving this house forever…And then the curtain would come down. It would be over.

Instead of all this waiting, waiting, like being sixteen again, wishing away that dead burden of time. Until this house is sold, she can never come of age. Julie's ghost is trapped inside the scent of coal tar soap, in the formica table tap and the lavatory pan webbed with little cracks. There are secret faces in the lino, hidden islands in the carpets. The scratchy boiled towels; the pale metal green caddy; the yellowed plastic fish slice – her mother used to whack her with that. That's for answering back. Frosted glass on the back door, a wobbly bolt, an awkward switch. Just a minute young lady, where do you think you're off to?

Nothing's ever thrown away and nothing changes. Judith's mother hates that cuckoo clock Aunt Edna gave her, but she still keeps it on the wall, twenty years since Edna died. The house is stuffed with wooden antelopes, elongated china cats, brass gongs, ashtrays with Blackpool written on them. The ceramic heads of Moors and Lascars still hang watchfully along the stairs. Only the fish are different, darting through the tank like sparks of coloured glass.

The place could have sold a year ago if they'd accepted the builder's offer – so what if he'd have made three times the price? Anything to be out of here for good. Peter's getting impatient. He's found somewhere he wants to buy, not far away, in fact, somewhere he's going to do up, him and his new girlfriend. He'll like that. He's always wanted to move out of the city.

Soon Judith will have no choice. She'll be forced to sell her own place and come here. The door will close behind her and the curtains will be drawn and every day will be a long grey February.

Judith's House
Delightful mid-terrace in popular part of S. Mcr. GCH. Modern Kitchen. Wooden floors. Small gardens, front and rear, planted

with mature shrubs. Must be seen to be appreciated.

Bare floorboards, Vera thinks, they look poverty-stricken. And the doors, they want a lick of paint, fancy leaving them like that. The house feels cold beneath the artificial heat. Like Julie herself, hard and cold. Surely to God she could get a carpet fitted. You could trip on them rugs.

Where's the tank going? No one's thought of that. You can't be too careful with fish, they don't like to be moved. This is all happening too quickly for Vera. Of course she's glad her house is sold at last. But she'd got used to the idea of staying put. Then the plans are changed again, solicitors are on your back, the phone's ringing, papers to be signed. She's told Julie, please yourself, she can't be mithered with it. It's one big racket anyway. Solicitors, surveyors – all after what they can get. If they had a man around that extension would be finished. Looks like she'll have to bring her chamber pot with her. Not that she couldn't manage the stairs if she had to. Julie's frightened she'll start mooching. As if Vera was interested. That's Julie all over. Cagey. Suspicious. We'll keep to our own space, she says, just as if we were in separate houses.

Vera's decided. 'I should like a red carpet down here. Something cheerful.'

Julie's lining up Vera's ornaments on the windowsill – the chimney sweep, the glass Bambi – piece by piece she brings them over, ready for the move. She turns to look fiercely at her mother. 'I can't go buying carpets. I've got a big loan on the extension and there'll be fees, you know, never mind what I'm giving to Peter.'

'It's my money,' Vera says, 'I slaved to buy that house.'

'The bed settee cost over a thousand pounds. Plus the van

hire....Ask Pam and Brian if you want carpets.'

Pam and Brian are buying off-plan in Turkey. Vera has stored that phrase in her mind. Buying off-plan, so their finances are rather tied up at the minute.

'If that settee cost a thousand, you were robbed.'

'Don't you believe me? I'll show you the receipt.'

Tight-fisted every one of them. Buying off-plan – typical Brian – all big ideas and nothing paid for. Even Carol with that great big television – everything on credit cards and loans. Tight-fisted and grasping and spoilt. Not one of them knows the true value of money, not one of them earns what they spend. All counting, no doubt, on getting their hands on her money, the little that's left, at some time not far off. What a surprise they've got coming. Just you wait, Vera thinks, just you wait till I'm dead.

Chapel of Rest

A quiet motel in some nowhere town you've never been, Telford say, or Ipswich, decorated with pastel striped wallpaper and swirling borders, in light blue and beige. Are the potted plants real or plastic? A pale girl with bad skin greets you at reception, leading you down the corridor, past closed doors towards the room where your mother is lying. Outside it's a blazing August day, thick with petrol fumes; in here the atmosphere's chilled and artificial, like the air inside a plane.

Behind the sunglasses, Judith's eyes are sore with weeping. She's rehearsed these scenes so many times, but now it's happening for real it all seems a bad joke. She always knew there'd be another fall or a heart attack, and that would finish her off – fairly quickly she hoped, without too much suffering. She thought quite coldly about all of that. What really happened was more prolonged and complicated. She was only being kept in for a few days as a precaution; and then, just as she was getting ready to leave she went down with MRSA.

The coffin's massive, the size of a wardrobe. Judith can't help this hysterical impulse to laugh – can't help herself – wanting to laugh as the girl slips away – almost square, you just don't expect that. She sits there a long time in the windowless room, before she's ready to do what she's come for.

This very week they should be in a caravan near Paignton. Judith was not looking forward to her so-called holiday. In fact she was dreading it. She had a chapter to finish on Almodovar; she needed some time to herself.

Well now, Vera says, you've got what you wanted. All the time in the world. You can please yourself now.

Judith's asked for the coffin lid to be left unscrewed so that when she's ready she can slide it along. She wasn't there when her mother died. No one was there. Pam was still in Turkey. No one knew the end was coming

When she's ready, Judith looks. And she tries to say goodbye.

Junk Shop

Judith's not interested in knickknacks. She's rummaging round half-heartedly for Ben's sake, while he stands nattering to the man behind the counter. Ben's good with people – that's one of the things she likes about him – but all they have is the weekend. She wants to get up on those hills before the weather changes.

Oh hurry up please – picking up commemorative plates and coffee pots and decorative tiles and putting them back down. There's nothing Judith wants, except maybe time, and that's not for sale. *Come on Ben.*

Then suddenly it's there. An ordinary biscuit tin, with two Dutch children on the lid. Her mother had one exactly like it years ago – kept her sewing stuff in it – cotton reels, needles, buttons and scissors. She's used to seeing bits of her childhood for sale – those big metal breadbins for instance, quite sought after now; blue green Tretchikoffs; bakelite egg cups. She's even kept one or two of these objects – a turquoise glass vase, a pair of elongated salad servers. Some small items went to her sisters, but most were quickly disposed off, sent to charity shops or thrown away Now all that old tat keeps coming back to haunt her, overpriced and slightly camp.

But the tin comes as a shock, not because it brings back any special trauma, just the opposite. There's no memory attached, nothing. It was completely forgotten, up to this moment, and yet it's more familiar than anything in her house in Manchester – the Dutch boy and girl striding hand in hand; the beige coloured lid, its roughened texture hinting at basketwork; a particular sort of nineteen-sixties roundness. What else has been lost, how much slipped her mind?

A giant safety pin, for fastening kilts. A wooden mushroom, meant for darning. A rusting metal thimble. A strip of name tags for school, her name – *Julie Bishop* – etched in green.

Look at this, Ben. But Ben's still engrossed. The talk's moved on to the confidential stage – tales of death, divorce and surgery, longstanding feuds and disputes over land. The black goatee and slant-rimmed glasses give Ben a Confucian air – the inscrutable judge. She'd never tell him this, but she used to be a little scared of Ben on conference panels – the booming

168

interventions, the sudden devilish laugh. In private, he's turned down a notch or two, gentler, unexpectedly tender, in this other incarnation. They have been an item for – how long? – nearly three months. He's becoming a fixture. *Hey Ben, look at this*...No, lets get out. Lets not dwell on the past.

Ben sees her and smiles. 'Hey, see what I got you.'

'Ben, please, don't go buying me presents. I don't want anything. I've too much stuff.'

'It's just a little something... I thought might amuse you.'

He hands her a Mexican *memento mori*, a small tableau, like a miniature stage set. A tiny doll is lying in bed, a skeleton lurking underneath, and a mirror behind, so you see your own face when you peer inside. *La Martina.*

'You wonder how it got here – how did it end up in a village in the Dales?'

'Thankyou,' she says, ashamed of herself

'You could put it on your desk and think of me.'

She smiles back at him bravely, tears starting in her eyes.

'Judith! Come on....' He gives her a squeeze, their cagoules rubbing awkwardly against each other. 'What is it? '

'Nothing.'

'Okay.... So you didn't find anything?' he says. 'Nothing take your fancy? Nothing at all?'

'No, I don't think so.'

Judith's life has changed completely since her mother died. She feels so much lighter, and the choices before her seem more simple and straightforward. But now and then that very lightness makes her dizzy and it's as if she's pretending, like she's going through the motions, as if she might look down and see the ground a thousand feet below.

'Come on,' she says, 'lets get out there before it starts raining.'

Eh Julie, I went such a thump. You should have seen me go flying.

COMPLETION

The next house they came to was a great gothic ruin. The House of the Seven Gables. The House of Usher. The House of the Dead. Hippies used to live there some time in the past – you could tell from the magenta paintwork, strangely pristine, like a thin skin barely masking the walls. Or not hippies exactly, Led Zeppelin freaks. Or Deep Purple, Pink Floyd or Santana. They held all-night parties here in the Court of the Crimson King, in the mythic times before Matt and Amy. They mounted their stereo – hey, cool – on the brick podium which oozed from an enormous feature fireplace. They helped themselves to booze from behind the brick bar, undulating all of one piece with the fire surround.

Matt and Amy were an item, made for each other. Amy thought she would never fall so easily again, until the day she spotted Matt waiting at a bus stop. And Matt worshipped Amy without letting her think she could walk on his wishes. Now they were going to live together, in some place in the country as yet undisclosed. It was Matt's belief that when they found that place they'd know. Just know. They'd fall in love at first sight.

Amy drew up a checklist. First of all, it had to be near a station, so Matt could get to work. Second, a garden for Amy's cat Edgar. Thirdly, a view for Amy herself The last house had been so lovely, with a perfect outlook, the velvety green landscape cascading down towards the sparkling river, and inside everything simple and ordered – the smooth plastered walls, the cast iron stove and the cellar, dry and neatly proportioned, so clean and perfect, and everything in its place, she felt delirious with desire. She had to hold still and remind herself, no garden, no garden, but what a view from the back, and so quiet – with the triple glazing you'd think you were in Eden, but no garden, Amy, nothing but a tiny yard between the front door and the road – the *main road*, Amy, you read me, *main road* – well maybe we could raise the wall – no don't be ridiculous – or put a balcony on the back – no, it's not going to work. She couldn't stop the mental cameras rolling, shooting blood and the bits of fur, half a second's carelessness, a door left on the latch, an open window... How could she sacrifice a living creature for a view? For property. That's all it was. Property. Bricks and mortar.

Reluctantly, she ruled out the house by the river. Yet the memory stayed with her through the day's viewings, like a first love, setting an impossible ideal. The contrast with this one could not have been greater.

We are pleased to offer this spacious mid-terrace, being located adjacent to railway station with links to Manchester and Leeds. The accommodation consists of... feature fireplace... telephone point... archway with sliding door to kitchen... enclosed bath with shower fitment... Every room contained something hideous. A purple bathroom suite. Fitted wardrobes gilded like King Ludwig's castle. Kitchen cupboards bodged from a dark, toxic wood in a Germanic style suitable for trolls or hobgoblins. Taps hammered into a plank balanced above the *single drainer stainless steel sink unit.* A plastic doll floating in grey water. These people had, finally, left in a rush. They had emptied the living spaces, but not finished clearing the kitchen. Something lingered, like a taste in the mouth. Amy was starting to feel a bit sick. She shouldn't have stayed up so late last night or drunk so much.

But once you reached the attic, all that décor dropped away. Nothing stood between the house and its architecture, not even the paisley patterns. You were inside the mind of the building. Matt braced his weight against the walls, testing the solidity of the ancient stone. He took in the polygonal shapes of the roofspace, thinking you might be in a castle or cathedral. Underneath all that crap, there was form and there was substance. You got plenty of space for your money, much more than that other house, the overdwelling, this was a substantial Victorian villa, an Englishman's home.

'Amy,' he said, 'hey look at this, doll. This could make a fantastic studio'

The lady from Boocock and Brown looked on. She picked up on that 'doll,' and Amy's slight flush when he said it. They were young. They had plenty of time.

'Don't you think?' He could see her already, hair pulled back in pigtails poised by the dormer window, sticking and cutting and pinning, pouring resin into moulds.

Amy specialised in what was known as non-functional clothing – thick, glassy slippers, dresses made out of the most friable fibres, loosely assembled and mounted like moths. She was currently artist in residence at the textile museum, where she showed school parties how to turn fruit into art. Amy was fascinated by skin, pith and peel. Dried oranges were preserved in the shoes, cucumbers and apple cores pressed into garments. Her first exhibition was sponsored by Cypressa, who donated cratefuls of lemons along with the dangerous brandy that got her into bed with Matt.

He was winning her round. She could see it too, the home that lay there waiting, that would become their own.

Anything bodged can be easily pulled down. Hard work, yes, but you could have a great time, get a few mates round, crates of beer, take a while, mucking in with hammers and chisels, yes, but it'd be worth it, think what you'd get. 'You could do one room at a time, work on it bit by bit, start at the top, and move down...'

They were young. They had all their lives before them. A long road ahead, with plenty to learn.

'I have to tell you,' said the woman, 'there's another couple interested. I don't know if they've put an offer in yet, but I shouldn't hang about if I was you.' Secretly, she was getting impatient. It was three o'clock already, nearly time to pick up her grandkids. This was a handy little job that she did, showing people round houses, and it brought in work for her husband if anyone needed a builder. She rarely gave her opinions, didn't need to. Houses sold themselves round here, even the most sorrowful, even the emptiest shell. And if she did say anything, people thought she was trying to trick them. They thought she was in cahoots with Boocock and Brown.

'Look,' he said, 'look,' pointing out the hills beyond the railway, and the small tangled garden, where a cat might safely roam.

But Amy had already seen exactly what he saw, and since he was so excited, she had to agree. He was the one who had not been so keen in the first place, who thought they should stay in the city.

Now he couldn't wait to put in an offer: 'You heard what she said.'

'Oh they always say there's some one interested. They'll call us. You'll see.'

174

Matt waggled his phone fretfully. The car had heated up while they were inside the house. The seats burned the backs of their legs, and even with the window open it was as if all the air had been stored in polythene. He stared into the busy street as they struggled out of the village. Three bookshops, two galleries, a wholefood café, a juice bar, innumerable pubs and dinky teashops, a magnet for daytrippers. No other word, a magnet. They'd despise the grockles down below when they were installed in their attic.

'Okay,' she said, 'go for it. Make a low offer.'

But he couldn't get a signal, and soon they were speeding down the motorway back towards home. They were almost at the turnoff when they hit the tailback. Tired and sweaty – they'd been looking at houses since breakfast – they sat glumly inside their little tin jail. A hot air balloon floated freely over the dreamy domes and turrets of the Trafford Centre and the pylons and ship canal and the great armoured wall of traffic down the M62.

Matt tried again, but it was already half past five. They'd all gone back to the places where estate agents live. 'I hate fucking August,' he said suddenly. Matt was like that. He was such a lovely guy, everybody liked him. They'd be amazed to know he could be so peevish – not often – but sometimes, and then it was gone so quickly, only those who loved him would have even noticed. And oh she did love him. She loved him so much. Mr. Business Man. Bringing home the bacon.

Her mind was made up. She could already picture herself in the Sunday supplements – a *restored Yorkshire – whatever – provides the perfect setting for an artistic couple –* yet still she kept hankering for that first house – the lettering

175

stamped on the stove, the nifty ladder to the attic; the radiant view across the river, framed by the window, like some eighteenth century painting. But Edgar had been with her since well before Matt. Unlovely, antisocial, he belonged to no one, but he'd stuck by her through the bad times, when no one else was there.

Some terrible crash up ahead. The story was on the news later, a minibus going to the airport, and two lorries jack-knifed across the middle lane. By the time they got to Amy's it was almost dark. The cat was squatting reproachfully on the windowsill waiting for his dinner, having spent an unsuccessful day foraging down the back alley.

This place was and was not the house they were buying. It wasn't the other house either. She was standing inside a walled garden, amongst lilies as tall as herself. Roses scrambled over the brickwork, washed pale by the moonlight.

In films and in books, dreams are all of a piece, like a story. But in Amy's dream the details were scattered. There was a pond with something in it, and a gate she couldn't close. Even as she fiddled with the lock, Amy knew she was asleep, and should save what she could for remembering later. But even that thought had to be fished out from her memory when her eyes opened. So much was unclear, amorphous. She wanted Matt to wake up before it all slipped away. He must have been there with her. How could he just sleep through?

But Matt lay still as death. He always slept soundly. He was uncomplicated. He didn't even stir as she went to open the window, half believing she'd see the garden down below. It was the Manchester street that seemed unreal to her – a TV screen pulsing through a lighted window, a couple shouting at each other from opposite sides of the road. All she wanted, at that moment, was to go back, to find her secret place.

He couldn't understand how she screwed up. So far as he could see she'd been on top of everything – checking out mortgages, talking to builders, even knocking the price down further when they got the survey back. She was the one who took everything on. She wanted to prove she could do it.

Amy was doing well for herself, selling one or two pieces every few months, and getting regular commissions. She was experimenting with courgettes, marrows and aubergines. She liked the cottony flesh of the aubergines – a fabric in itself – but preserving them was tricky. She gave up on her original plan, to use overlapping circles, in favour of a mosaic effect – purplish tiles on a muslin ground, making a kind of bodice, something almost military she thought, like armour. And that was when the phone went.

'This is Virginia Howe.' The voice rang icy with rage. 'What exactly do you think you're playing at?'

'Sorry?' Amy was petrified. She had no idea who this person could be.

'When I accepted your offer, it was for an early completion. That was over two months ago. I thought you were first time buyers. I could have sold that house twenty times over.'

'It's all ready, the searches are done, the mortgage offer just has to come through.'

'The mortgage offer.' The voice grunted in disgust. 'I've had it with you. You've made your bed.'

Mrs. Howe, the mysterious Vendor. They had never communicated directly till then. Everything was done through solicitors and estate agents, and Amy somehow imagined unexplained tragedies sending her into seclusion. Now she felt weak with terror. Everything was crumbling beneath her.

At last she got hold of Matt at a sales conference in Oslo, Oslo, of all the far places the company chose to send him.

'Amy,' he said, 'I wish you'd told me that. You didn't tell me you agreed to a quick completion.'

She remembered now, when she put in an offer, the estate agent used exactly that expression, and when Amy asked how soon, she said 'just quick'; and so Amy thought it was just one of those things people say. You know. To save face when accepting an offer.

'Yes, but Amy, you entered into a commitment. Without informing me. All this time, I've been acting under false assumptions.'

'It always takes ages when you buy a house.'

'No it doesn't, not always. If you instruct the solicitor properly, you can do it in weeks. Listen Amy, we're in charge. Solicitors, estate agents – they're supposed to work for us. Have you got a number for this woman? No. Okay. 1471 – I'll ring you back. Let me talk to her. And tell that solicitor to get off his arse. Right now, Amy. Make sure you get through.'

You entered into a commitment, Amy. He never spoke to her like that before.

Always called her doll, *hey doll, come here....* It was because he was with those men in suits. He was acting like them. He was one of them, standing round some conference suite in their steel rimmed glasses. One of them, the grown-ups, the people who ran the world, who made the rules. She was on her own. All alone, crying so hard she couldn't make the phone call to the solicitor. She had to pretend. It was the first lie she ever told him.

He apologised when he called back for the number. 'I'm sorry doll, I didn't mean to shout at you.'

'You weren't shouting.' That was true. He never raised his voice.

'I miss you like fuck'.

'It's all my fault...'

'Don't talk about the house, it doesn't matter babe, it'll sort itself out. Trust me, okay? Just tell me what you're up to. What you do today?'

Like I was a little girl. Tell Daddy what you did.

Missed her so bad. Could have trashed the hotel room, wrecked the cool empty beds, smashed his own smug reflection in the sterile bathroom. He wanted to be himself again. Wanted to be home. This house or that, what did it matter? So long as nothing changed between them, and she was still his little Amy. His sexy little doll. Outside the window, the night was sharp and clear. Not long, he told himself, not long, we'll be together, and in a year or two I'll ask her to marry me and then we'll have children, a boy and a girl.

Back in Manchester, the moon was buried under clouds. In the weeks leading up to Bonfire Night, fireworks thudded every few minutes like a report from the Somme. Time was slipping away from her – Halloween, Christmas, New Year rolling on towards her birthday at the end of January – twenty-nine, nearly thirty, moving on to forty, fifty, soon be dead, they'd both be dead. When Amy finally got to sleep, she dreamt she couldn't stop the car, the white Polo she drove to classes and craft shows. Her foot kept sliding off the pedal. In her waking hours, she dreaded hearing that icy voice again. She was so afraid, she let the landline ring unanswered and kept her mobile switched off. The voice of the Vendor still spoke in her ear, catching her whenever she was off guard. *'What do you think you're playing at?'* Stupid, how could she be so stupid? Nothing worked. The little squares of aubergine kept dropping off the canvas.

Of course the woman was bluffing when she threatened to call off the sale. Matt knew that instinctively. The house would have been theirs, if they just kept their nerve. But Amy had fallen out of love with the ruined Victorian villa. To be honest, she'd never been one hundred per cent certain, she'd just convinced herself, because Matt was so keen. But think of all that work, stretching on for months and years...Maybe Mrs. Whatsit had done them both a favour. Matt agreed; there'd be other houses.

And there were. Within a fortnight of the Vendor pulling out, they found an ex-council house up on the heights with fantastic views and a garden for Edgar; the only downside was the slog from the station, but that didn't matter. They could live with it, Matt said. The sale went through without a hitch; everyone knew that the market was turning. By springtime Amy was stripping doors and sewing curtains.

This house had no history. Inside, it was an empty box, the walls painted vanilla, with vertical blinds at the windows and laminate floors. The fitted kitchen had never been used. Even so, there were doors that wouldn't shut, leaks in the sink, missing tiles, things they'd missed that were obvious once you moved in. One day when Matt was at work, Amy decided she couldn't stand the woodchip in the bedroom any longer. Leaving the resin to harden round the leathery skins of figs, she set to with the wallpaper stripper. She knew it was madness, but something possessed her. She took down all the pictures – her aubergine composition; Matt's photos from Prague and Barcelona – and flung plastic sheeting over the furniture.

Soon she was completely absorbed, steaming the paper and pulling it off in sheets, like peeling skin, building up a rhythm to Goldfrapp and PJ Harvey, playing all the music she liked and Matt didn't. It was easier than she thought; there were no other layers underneath the first. Imagine doing this in the other house. But in the first house she wouldn't have had to change anything. The ladder wobbled as she reached into a corner. *Amy,* Matt warned in her head, and was disregarded. She sang along to Madonna. The cat looked on, disgusted.

She liked the warm, fleshy colour of raw plaster. Maybe they'd keep it like that. *Provides the perfect setting for an artistic couple.* She'd nearly stripped the whole room, except the ceiling. Best leave the ceiling. She'd done all round the window – UPVC, but it was practical, Matt said, if unaesthetic. The last stretch proved the most difficult. One wall hadn't been replastered. To start with it wasn't too bad, but as she neared the door chunks of grey stuff fell away as she wrenched the paper free. Suddenly, she saw exposed brickwork, and a scar the shape of lightning running straight through it. The crack was so deep she could've put her hand in, if she dared. It was so deep she went outside, frightened of the house collapsing.

But of course it wouldn't. The woodchip wasn't holding up the walls; if she hadn't stripped the paper, she wouldn't have known the crack was there. Now the day was nearly gone. Matt was on his way home. By the time he arrived she'd have to clear up the rubble and sour-smelling woodchip, store the ladder and the stripper, and put all the furniture back into place, making sure that something covered the crack so at least they wouldn't have to think about it. Her own stupid fault for not leaving things be. She'd made her own bed, and now she'd have to lie in it. She opened the window and looked down the valley, hoping he wouldn't be cross because she couldn't bear for him to be cross with her ever.

END OF STORY

Not many people know that Ned's been married. They think he's probably a virgin. Yet twenty years ago Ned was passionately in love. At that time his research into glottochronology was only one of his interests. He fished at weekends, he was learning the fiddle and reading medieval romances from the courtly tradition. There's always been something boyish about Ned's enthusiasms – his enjoyment, for instance, of every kind of kit and tackle – chisels, knives and trowels, farmyard tools and rods and flies. At that stage in his life, Ned saw himself as a countryman and had spent his trust fund on a tumbledown farm in the part of Lancashire said to have inspired Tolkien's Middle Earth.

Ned came into a tidy sum of money when he was twenty-one. His mother was bought off by his father soon after he was born, on condition that she severed all contacts. Ned had no idea who his father was, and his identity remains one of the very few subjects in which he shows not even a theoretical curiosity.

He hadn't been farming long before he fell in love with a tragic widow. The tale of her husband's death is too complex to relate; and in fact she was not quite a widow since her husband had remarried, but so far as she was concerned the divorce was immaterial. Even now, you might imagine what she saw in Ned, once you had mentally shorn off his beard, straightened his glasses, and spruced him up; you could see how he might have won her over with his tremendous eagerness and the spaniel like devotion he had to offer, and the prospect of the two of them, together, making a go of the farm, in that lovely spot, abandoned all those years, imagine her orphaned children

– and more children to come – helping feed the chickens, and perhaps – for Nancy was practically minded and this was her suggestion – a campsite on the field by the stream, and even bed and breakfast.

You can imagine how Ned loved his Nancy and how he would do anything for her. Except get out of the armchair on a Sunday morning when he was doing the crossword. Or leave his chatting to some old biddie in the post office to get back to the cowshed. Or put those musty old books to one side when the roof needed sorting. Ned was born to be a bachelor. He could not put a lid back on a jar or close a drawer or pick up a sock from the floor, let alone clear out a barn or mend a roof. When she mentioned a fence that needed fixing, he'd say, 'The whole lot needs replacing.'   But he wouldn't do anything about replacing it, apart from wandering round the suppliers admiring different types of fence. The small jobs weren't worth bothering with, and the big ones had to be thought through and planned. He couldn't just go outside and do it, now could he?

He drove her mad.

Most of the windows were still boarded up. If she'd been able to look out, the views over the fells would have cheered her. On a clear day you could make out Blackpool Tower in the distance, and glimpse the sea. But the only windows with glass in them faced onto the rotting outbuildings, and the dumped washing machines and rusting machinery which should have been cleared by the previous owner. Ned never stood up for his rights – something else that annoyed her.

One winter's day, the next door farmer rapped on the door. He wouldn't come inside; his boots were thick with mud. 'Where's your husband?' he said. 'Something I want to show him.'

Ned was in town, fetching some heavy duty rubble sacks, which meant he'd be away for hours, dawdling round the second hand bookshop.

'I'll go,' she said.

'No, you'd better not. You don't want to see this.'

Two of his calves had fallen into the septic tank. He wanted compensation. He was polite, insistent, but not angry. Nancy was angry.

'I told you,' she raged at Ned, 'you should have fixed the bloody fence. And what's the cover doing off the tank? Christ, Ned…What if the kids…'

'Nancy my love, he's trying it on. Those calves weren't worth tuppence. Have you seen how he keeps his animals? The field's churned with mud, he crams in too many, he's ruining the pasture, no wonder they come over our side. And for your information, the cover was closed.'

'You're not saying he put them in himself?'

Ned shrugged, puffing at the Meerschaum pipe he'd bought on his trip into town, having felt a sudden impulse to experiment with smoking. 'Nancy, let me take care of it. You don't know farming and you don't know farmers. End of story.'

She had been cheated. This was not a partnership. Life on the so-called farm, a yard with a few chickens and a superannuated sheepdog was not what she'd been promised when she agreed to marry. Ned did nothing about speaking to their neighbour, and after his second visit, she simply took out the chequebook and forged Ned's scrappy signature next to her own. He never noticed, despite his pretence that he was keeping the accounts when he was mooching about in his office. She forged his signature again, whenever she felt she was entitled to a new dress or a hairdo. (Such fripperies were considered an extravagance, unlike Germanic tomes on glottochronology.)

She had tried to use her feminine wiles. 'I'm worried about that pond – what if the children – do you think that wiring is safe – if ever the twins were to touch it...' She tried having a go herself, hoping he'd come to her rescue. But Ned was oblivious. Lost in his books, he didn't even hear her shrieks when she banged her thumb with the hammer After the septic tank incident, she turned to emotional blackmail. 'Ned, this place is dangerous. The kids can't stay here, not unless you do something about it' and then to outright threats. 'If you don't get your act together, the kids are going to have to stay with their grandparents.'

Ned had a soft spot for children. He was a child himself. But her threats made no difference. She packed them off 'temporarily' while the farm was, as she put it, 'being renovated,' and the place was, at least, quieter without them. Apart from that bloody dog. She got out of the house more and more, going horse-riding and signing up for classes on aromatherapy and massage at the community centre.

Even so, the time came when she could stand it no longer. As she listened for Ned's tread on the wonky staircase, his farts and belches on his way to join her, some greasy book in hand, she knew she couldn't share a bed with him again. Since their marriage, he'd stopped trimming his beard and sometimes forgot to clean his teeth. He stank of exotic pipe tobacco. Sex was out of the question, though he didn't seem to mind. He always left it to her to make the first move.

She slipped out of the bedroom and into what had been

the twins' room. Where could she go? There was nowhere. She had nothing. Her first husband left her penniless. There was no way she was going back into nursing and no other job she could do.

'Nancy, my love? What are you doing?' He had a light and pleasant voice, a kind voice. 'Sweetness?'

The door was locked.

'You're not coming in,' she said. 'We're finished. I mean it. I'll live upstairs and you live downstairs. You use the back door and I'll use the front.'

Ned played along, convinced she'd change her mind. After all, he'd done nothing wrong. He'd been a good husband. He'd soon win her round. But the flowers he left every day at the foot of the stairs were left untouched, until they were as parched as potpourri. He became more and more involved with his glottochronology, poring over his books through the night and sleeping till mid-day and then perhaps driving into town for a sandwich at The Bull. The dog's ears might occasionally prick at the click of a latch, or the sound of the chickens cackling as she fed them, but he never came face to face with his beloved Nancy.

Sometimes he could tell that she had been downstairs. She was like the fairies; things went missing now and then. A pair of scissors or some change from the windowsill. The fiddle had been dusted off and moved to one side in the hallway.

Things took a turn for the worse one lunchtime on a beautiful Spring day, and it was all over something quite trivial really. Ned couldn't find the keys to the van. He hunted everywhere – through piles of old newspapers, in the tangle of bedding on the sofa, under the carpet. At this rate, The Bull would have finished serving, and besides today he had a specially urgent reason to eat there, because one of the regulars had promised to talk to him about the cattle auction. Ned hated any disruption to his routine, but he was especially looking forward to telling Nancy about this encounter, just to prove that he was doing some serious research into livestock. (Not that they were actually speaking at all, except in the long conversations he held in his head.)

'Nancy!' he bellowed in desperation. 'Nancy!'

He charged upstairs. He knew she had them, from the way the van was parked. Nancy was one of those women who hated driving, but would get in the car now and then when she had to, and you could tell from the skewed angle of the old Morris van that she'd been into town.

He was halfway through the door before she had a chance to slam it against him.

'What are you doing?' she said.

'Come on,' he said, 'this is ridiculous.'

'You do not come up here,' she said. 'You do not come near me.'

She spoke with such venom he was momentarily paralysed.

'But where's it all leading?' he begged her. 'What's going on?'

'If you want to ask me anything, put it in writing. You don't come storming up here, threatening and shouting.'

'I see,' he said. But he didn't.

Put it in writing. So night after night he sat laboriously typing out letters, posting them on his way to the Bull. On her birthday he even sent a parcel, waking early in the morning to hear the postman's knock. The first letter was returned 'not known at this address,' but she thought better of it, and he imagined her keeping them all, smiling at his little jokes. He saw himself as a chevalier put to the test, winning his lady through perseverance, and he started addressing her in the letters as 'My dearest Griselda, plus tendres d'un herenc.'

And then she began to taunt him, like a poltergeist. Books went missing. A string was broken on the fiddle. For several days, his morning lie-ins were disturbed by some kind of banging and bumping; so far as he was concerned, she could redecorate as she pleased, but whatever she was up to – and let her get on with it – there was no need for quite such a racket. It was hard to imagine that she'd be so petty or what he'd done to deserve so much spite. He'd left her alone, hadn't he? Perhaps that was it; she was provoking him. He'd been too considerate. She wanted him to show her who was boss.

It was a very bad summer, too wet to go fishing or do anything outdoors. He lingered in the Bull on those long afternoons, declaiming his opinions and exchanging bar room lore. He was like a terrier once he got his teeth into a subject; and he was well informed on every topic. Sometimes it was nearly dark before he went home. If you could call it home. That evening the sky was purple with the imminent storm. Coming up the drive, he felt a pang at the sight of her lighted window. His Rapunzel. And then he realized.

He could see inside. He could see the pale glow of the walls and the bookshelves lined with candles and potions. But that window had been boarded up. What *had* she been doing? Standing outside, he understood how shallow and tasteless, how utterly fatuous, she could be. Nancy had installed a cheap PVC window in a seventeenth century farmhouse.

He was so angry he could barely turn the key in the front door. 'Nancy,' he roared, 'Nancy, this has got to stop.'

There was no response. He forged ahead, taking the stairs two at a time. 'I have a right to my own house. I'm coming upstairs and I'm going to spend the night there.'

Suddenly she was there on the dim landing, hair wet, in her dressing gown.

'Don't you threaten me,' she said.

He said, 'This game is over. I don't know what you're playing at –'

'Ha!' she laughed.

What happened next was disputed. Ned said he took a step towards her, she recoiled and backed into the banister; Nancy that he pushed her aside to get into the bedroom. Both agreed that if he had got around to replacing the stair rails then the accident wouldn't have happened. So either way you looked at it, her injuries were caused by Ned. Miraculously she had nothing more than severe bruising and a broken arm. In those long seconds on the way down, he was convinced that she'd die, and all he felt at the foot of the stairs was relief, mingled with fear, and as he drove to the hospital through the dark torrential rain great waves of love and a desire for redemption. He would take care of her. He would nurse her back to health.

There was no chance of that. Her friend Janet, from the aromatherapy class, was summoned almost instantly, and during her two week stay Janet turned into a go-between, informing Ned that while Nancy wasn't going to press charges she was asking for an injunction, keeping him out of the house. She was starting divorce proceedings immediately.

As Ned explained at the Bull, Nancy could spin a yarn. Asked how they first got together, he'd simply say, 'Nancy told a good story.' (He didn't want to speak about the 'Learning to Love Yourself' workshop.) The typed letters formed part of the case against him; he had described her as a *'belle dame sans merci'* using what Nancy's solicitor took to be threatening language. Photocopied sections were sent to him, the quotations highlighted in yellow.

Tristrans murut pur sue amur

E la bele Ysolt par tendrur.

What did that mean? Was it a death threat?

Janet testified that, on a previous occasion, Nancy had shown her bruises on her arms, and that Janet had advised her to go to the doctor, who verified that Nancy was under extreme stress and living in fear of her husband. Even before the relationship broke down she had been obliged to send her children away since her husband wilfully refused to make the farm habitable.

What bruises? Which occasion? Had he grabbed hold of her, trying to make her look at him, to listen? When she hid the car keys? Because she did hide those keys, he was certain. It occurred to him that she might have bruised herself riding, but by then it was too late.

She said he was paranoid, accusing her of damaging the property and changing his mind about improvements he had sanctioned. He had spoken about living as a hermit; in one of the letters he had written: 'We shall live as true bohemians, free spirits who care not for worldly things. What is material comfort? What does it matter?'

And so on for twenty pages.

'I could tell a story,' he said, thinking of his broken fiddle. 'I could tell a tale or two.'

'Why don't you?' they said at the Bull.

'Because I am a gentleman.'

And because he still loved her. He could never give that up.

When the divorce came through he was instructed to take the farm to sealed bids, handing over half his assets to Nancy. If he'd made a go of the place, he could have argued that he was losing his business. But the court decided it was not a working farm, it was the marital home, and besides there were children to provide for. Everything happened so quickly and yet it also took forever – meeting with solicitors, filling in forms, waiting for signatures, making inventories and, worst of all, clearing the farm once contracts were exchanged.

Nancy lived there right up to completion. He avoided entering the house when there were signs of her presence, concentrating instead on getting rid of the conked-out freezers and rusty engines and other debris, evicting the feral cats and clearing the henhouse. These days Nancy had her own little Fiat, and when it was gone, sometimes for days on end, he went inside to fetch the remainder of his books, those not sold or given to the church bazaar. Once he considered searching upstairs; he was halfway up, the boards creaking underfoot, when he thought he heard a car pull up and changed his mind. He'd never laboured so hard as those last few weeks – so caught up in the physical effort that he had no room left for grief or nostalgia, not even on his final trip when he looked for the last time at the land that was his.

He seemed quite contented living in his caravan,

wandering down to the Bull at lunchtimes and reading into the night. He was turning away from his countryman phase towards the life of a scholar. Even the loss of so many books didn't bother him unduly. He had what he needed, and that was enough.

The only other thing he'd taken from the farmhouse was the old sheepdog. Round about one o'clock every day you'd see the pair of them together, Prince wheezing and grumbling in a heap at the foot of the bar stool while Ned made his pronouncements on the state of the nation. Poor old chap, his back legs were giving way. Prince always had problems getting up stairs, but now he could barely drag himself from the caravan. His eyes were glazed, his coat was grey and matted, and even Ned caught the whiff from his fur as he lifted him into the van.

And then one day Ned was on his own, supping his pint without a word, sitting at a corner table. 'Reckon this'll be the end of Thatcher,' some one ventured and then – 'what she wants is another Falklands.' The regulars glanced over at Ned, waiting for him to expand on the subject but he just smiled back weakly, and left half an hour later, his beer unfinished and his sandwiches untouched. The landlady reckoned there were tears in his eyes when he ordered. But there was no one else to notice. And he was back to his old self by the time Kuwait was invaded.

The Bull's changed hands several times since then. It's a gastropub now, and Ned's old farm is a thriving equestrian centre. He never goes back; he's not interested. He's become the man he is now, discarding the past like the shell that hatched him, a fully self-sufficient species, one of a kind. He no longer has any wish to belong; home is just a place to store your books.

And there are many of them, thousands, piled on floors and blocking doors and windows in the house he rents in town. As he always told Nancy, you can never have too many books.

There is one in particular he is keeping an eye on, a field study of the Bahnaric Mon-Khmer languages of Vietnam undertaken by Spielhagen in 1934, a rare copy of which has just appeared second hand on Amazon – his copy, he's certain, stolen by Nancy. *Dispatched from MD, United States international delivery rates available.* 'Despatch' is his own preferred usage, though this is one of those unusual instances where English offers two parallel spellings. Buying your own books back is rather annoying, even if they are ridiculously underpriced. But it's only money. What does he have to lose?

DOORS OF TUNIS

I don't know where the hell we're going. I was meant to give directions. Nick's car blunders through the back streets in the hinterland between Rusholme and Fallowfield, one blind corner rounding into another. I'll be late for my class. Late and screwed up. Screwed up and late.

Silence between us. Time to draw another weapon. 'That poster you brought back for me...'

'Which poster?'

'Doors of Tunis. You got it for nothing, didn't you? There's a logo, ATB bank, at the bottom.'

'There you are again,' Nick says wearily, 'you're so cynical sometimes. I spent hours, hours, walking round the Medina, looking for something to bring you.'

'Sorry.' I touch his thigh, forbidden now.

'That was a shitty thing to say.' He pauses dramatically. 'And one of those doors was open.'

5.51 p.m., and at last we've reached the highway. Now it's straight down the curry mile. Past the Mughlai and the Darbar, onto Oxford Road, past the Infirmary and Manchester Uni. and Manchester Met. and the College of Music, over the edge of the city centre, heading for the finish, on this, the eleventh day of the eleventh month, shortly after the end of British Summer Time, our seventh month together, which turns out to be the last.

I look at him now while I still can, his iron profile hard as the head on a coin. 'Why do you think I say those things?'

Because you're afraid. Because you love me.

But the answer he gives is not the right one. And he

doesn't turn to face me, not even for a second, while we're waiting for the signals to change by the Contact Theatre. Heavy traffic. Brake lights shine through the glossy darkness. But there's not far to go, now he knows where he is.

5.53 – I'll be early after all. I check again that I've packed my notes and handouts, the right DVD. And my glasses.

An hour ago, this morning, last week, I felt safe. Crossing the park on Halloween, the leaves sizzling under the sharp winter sun, I thought, *There's some one thinking of me*; fifty miles away, some one thought of me sometimes. Nick would be finishing his visits, climbing back inside the car, locking the door, and lighting one of the cigarettes that he forbade his patients. It was during this time that, once, a half-dressed woman banged on the window, screaming that her baby wouldn't wake up. She'd given him methadone to make him go to sleep. Alexander, the child was called. Poor Little Alex.

There were other stories, but I didn't hear them often. Just working, he'd say, when I asked what he'd been up to. Birth, disease and death – the usual. His silence was terrible sometimes. But I told myself not to be scared by the sudden absence in his eyes or by his voice, cold and remote at the dead end of the line – because he always came back to himself in the end. Back to me. For a moment, in All Saints Park, the world kept still, balanced by that certainty.

I tell him: 'You need some one fat and jolly. Some one to jolly you along.' I say this because I'm thin, because whatever else is lacking at least I'm slim and waspish.

'Some one to mother me?' he says, searching for a

parking spot. 'And what about you, what do you need?'

I need you.

It's just after six. I don't start teaching till half past. Time's slowed down since he turned up, slowed down as it does in those attenuated moments when you know there's going to be an accident.

When he turned up, I said: 'Nick! What you doing here? You forgot, it's my evening class on Tuesday nights. Hey Nick, I've got *Orphee*, we can watch it on Friday after *Coronation Street...*'

He said: 'I've got something to tell you. I met some one.'

Not some one else, but some one. I felt a coldness bite between my ribs.

'Well, not met exactly – I met her a couple of years ago – but she was at the garage – I'd just run out of matches and Abdul's was shut...'

'What do you mean? I don't understand what you're talking about.'

Putting the kettle on. Getting milk out the fridge. This afternoon, round about five, as the Betware catalogue slipped through the letterbox, and the ice cream van came round, playing *Anchors Aweigh*. What garage?'

6.03: the Java. Nick likes cafés, takeaways and coffee bars. He even treats McDonald's like the Ritz. The board offers cappuccino, espresso, latte, Americana, mocha. 'What do you recommend?' he asks the girl behind the counter, 'is it good?' She answers diffidently; after all, it's only coffee. He turns to me: 'Sure you don't want a bun or something? You don't eat enough.'

I know I'll never walk in here again without remembering. Whenever I hear Gershwin playing in the background my heart will start to bleed. The espresso machine splutters, and Louis Armstrong hisses, '*Besssss, you is my woman now...*' and the music slowly gathers strength behind him, waiting for Ella's gracious reply.

The Spanish-looking guy in the corner's reading his *El Pais*. He's always in here – probably thinks I am too; in fact he looks up, almost nods, as we sit down.

Nick finds his fags. I wonder if she smokes – *she*, that whisper snaking through my brain. Bet she smokes grass like Nick – some rolling, braying hippy that he can get stoned with, and reminisce about the sixties.

I tell him, 'Your cough's getting worse.'

'Just the standard old man's hack.'

'You sound like the Lady of the Camellias. You want to get some central heating at your place.'

'Don't need to. I'm a stoic. I've been to boarding school.'

At the next table, a man and woman are facing each other. A little crucifix swings in his ear. 'I would not let anyone talk to me in that loose way from a funding body,' he announces. The only person I've let do that is what's-her-name from Combined Arts.'

'I know what you're saying.'

'Here's the space, we know the rules, this as much money as I need, de da, de da – that's all you need to put across.'

'I know.'

'It's simple.'

Nick holds a cup with his left hand, although he's mostly

right handed. He always leaves an inch or two at the bottom. He sleeps flat on his back, arms folded on his chest like a stone effigy. In the mornings, he pretends not to be awake. My fingers creep gently round his thighs then he groans, *if I must – you're insatiable – I know I'm just a sex object.* On the night the clocks went forward we passed dark chocolate from our mouths like a bird feeds its young. We fed on one another.

'It wasn't going anywhere was it?' he says. 'Come on. Be honest. I got on your nerves. You were bored. You hated staying at home watching telly. You despise television, in your heart, admit it. I don't mind the cinema once in a while, but all this gangster stuff, it makes me sick. It's degrading. Lets face it Nancy, we're incompatible.'

'What's the television got to do with anything? You just don't fancy me any more.'

'No, that's not it. That's not it.'

'You'd sooner fuck some one else. What's the point in going over things? It's finished. You dumped me. So what if you feel guilty? Don't rationalise.'

'Do you want me to go?'

'No, it's okay.' How else to kill time? Nineteen minutes left, then I'll step in front of the class, trim and sharp and on the spot. Oh, I'll be good tonight. For two short hours this dream will be suspended.

'What're you doing with them this time?'

'You'd love it,' I tell him sarcastically. 'It's right up your street. Hitchcock, *Vertigo*, remember? Jimmy Stewart forces Kim Novak to dress up like another woman. Then he drives her to her death.'

To my surprise, he does remember; Nick's film taste

coalesced in the film societies of the sixties, with fuzzy prints of Bergman, Fellini, Kurosawa. I don't quite believe him when he tells me he saw *Vertigo* when it came out. It seems far too long ago, another age. He was alive before I was born.

'My father took me – must have been in the fifties some time.'

'1958 – you were seven.' Suddenly I'm looking at him, Nick – not some man, some stranger, but Nick, Nick – don't you know me?

'That's a weird thing to take a child to see.'

His face seems to soften as he glances through my notes, making comments, offering suggestions. That's Nick – he knows something about everything, or so he pretends. Fatherly Nick, Nick the nice doctor. Hello Nancy, he says, his voice posh and controlled. Hello Nancy, it's me, what you up to? Finished marking yet? Oh, I'm just sitting here, you know, just chilling for five minutes. Just sent out the last patient. You should see this place, you know, you should visit. There's metal grilles on the windows, and when the sun's in the right position you get shadows just like spiders' webs on the wall. You'd like it. Very *film noir*.

Hello Nancy – that slow, precise way he speaks my name – hello Nancy. Just the usual – birth, disease and death. Listen, I could come over to Manchester later. If you're not busy, that is. Nick hates farewells. He never wants a goodbye kiss. It reminds him of being sent to school, the whole family standing on the platform until at last the whistle blew and he could go inside. On its way through London, the train went past his house. His parents might be back home already, listening to the news, feeding the dog, as if he'd never existed. He could almost see his Airfix models hanging in the bedroom window.

Nick, it's me; don't you know me? I nearly take his hand. I almost say, this is stupid, there is no other woman, you're making it all up. But it's too late. Twenty-five past six.

When I come out of the toilet, he's vanished. My big empty coat's sitting in the chair, the sleeves concertina'ed where I pulled my arms free. I wish I could escape. Maybe there's another exit, but of course there isn't. I can see him waiting on the street, his back against the window. Putting on my coat seems somehow complicated. I watch my bag overbalance, the DVDs clattering to the floor.

The arts couple are splitting the difference. Some one else is sitting in the Spanish guy's place, and Miles Davis is playing 'So What'. The girl behind the counter smiles at me on my way out. Nick always leaves a generous tip.

Sometimes he looks so defeated. I wish I knew how to help him. He looks so old sometimes. He's standing there in his Rupert Bear scarf like a dim reflection, an arm's length away, stubbing out another half-smoked cigarette. One minute to go. What happens now? Do lovers shake hands at the end of the match? Do we embrace like shipmates, bidding farewell? Or kiss for one last time, surreptitiously warming ourselves on the heat stored in our bodies?

'It wasn't all bad, was it?' he says. 'I know I'm hard to get on with – but we had some good times, didn't we?'

'I suppose so.' I shrug. 'Well then, see you' – except that's the wrong expression, because I know I shan't, not ever. I turn down the street proudly without looking back. I'm walking fast. I'm walking fast towards my class to stop myself from falling.